Freya picked up the top newspaper and scanned the headlines.

She saw the photograph of her and Nash before she could comprehend the accompanying title. Distress was clearly evident on her shocked face, but it was Nash's heart-stopping visage that riveted her even more. The photograph had captured him with his arm tightly circled round her waist, and he looked both possessive and fierce. All the moisture seemed to dry up inside her mouth.

'I got up early to go and get those.' Nash jerked his head towards the newspaper. 'I wanted to see what they'd write.'

'And? Wait… Don't tell me. No doubt it's something along the lines of "has-been actress falls down drunk in the street"!' Was there no end to this torment of mind, body and soul? Resigned, she waited for Nash to tell her the worst. Her French was fairly inadequate, and there was just a minimal amount of words she understood.

'It's nothing like that.'

'Then what is it?'

'They're suggesting that you and I are lovers.'

The day **Maggie Cox** saw the film version of *Wuthering Heights,* with a beautiful Merle Oberon and a very handsome Laurence Olivier, was the day that she became hooked on romance. From that day onwards she spent a lot of time dreaming up her own romances, secretly hoping that one day she might become published and get paid for doing what she loves most! Now that her dream is being realised, she wakes up every morning and counts her blessings. She is married to a gorgeous man, is the mother of two wonderful sons, and her two other great passions in life—besides her family and reading/writing—are music and films.

Recent titles by the same author:

THE MILLIONAIRE BOSS'S BABY
THE SPANIARD'S MARRIAGE DEMAND

PUBLIC MISTRESS, PRIVATE AFFAIR

BY
MAGGIE COX

MILLS & BOON
Pure reading pleasure

First published in Great Britain 2007
Harlequin Mills & Boon Limited,
Eton House, 18-24 Paradise Road, Richmond, Surrey TW9 1SR

© Maggie Cox 2007

ISBN: 978 0 263 85369 8

Set in Times Roman 10½ on 13 pt
01-1107-43845

Printed and bound in Spain
by Litografia Rosés, S.A., Barcelona

PUBLIC MISTRESS, PRIVATE AFFAIR

CHAPTER ONE

'NASH! Good to see you, my friend. Thanks for dropping by at such short notice. I know you're a very busy man.'

His hand was gripped by the bearlike clasp of the tall, dark-eyed, bearded giant in front of him, and Nash Taylor-Grant's answering smile was brief but relaxed. 'No problem. You'd better tell me what all this is about.'

'I'll get my secretary to bring us in some coffee first.'

'You go ahead, but I'll take a rain-check, if you don't mind.' Nash grimaced as he peeled off his expensive coat and sat down in one of the leather club chairs opposite the long polished desk. 'Cutting down on the caffeine,' he offered laconically.

Nash hadn't known Oliver Beaumarche long, but in the relatively short time they'd been acquainted it had become clear that the wealthy and successful restaurateur was to be a good friend. Having regularly dined at both his upmarket London restaurants—for business and for pleasure—Nash didn't hesitate to recommend the establishments to his other well-connected friends whenever the opportunity arose.

Now Oliver had asked for Nash's help in a professional capacity, and although he hadn't hesitated to assure him that of course he would help, in whatever way he could, Nash was perplexed as to why the older man would need the kind of expertise that he particularly excelled in. 'Damage limitation' was how his stock in trade was known in the PR business—the protection of famous clients' reputations in the media—and it had made Nash's fortune. And, whilst Oliver Beaumarche was a respected and well-known name in the world of high-profile eateries, he was hardly an A-list or even B-list celebrity—and as far as Nash was aware he hadn't been involved in any scandal lately that would make his reputation in need of rescuing.

'Well, then.' Following his lead, Oliver lowered his large, impressive frame into a wing-backed chair and sighed heavily. 'Someone I very much care about has been going through the most horrendous situation and needs some help. Unfortunately it's not the kind of help that I can deal with on my own, and that's why I need to talk to you.'

His lightly tanned brow furrowing, Nash leant forward in his seat, loosely linking his hands together as he thoughtfully surveyed the other man. 'It all sounds a bit of a mystery, if you don't mind my saying. You know what I do…so how can I help?'

'The girl I'm talking about is my niece…my sister Yvette's only child. I'm afraid I've rather doted on her since she was a baby, and when she lost her father when she was only six—I suppose I took on a paternal role in her life.'

'You aren't making this any clearer, my friend.' Now it was Nash's turn to sigh. As much as he respected the other man, and genuinely wanted to be of assistance if he could, he had practically back-to-back appointments waiting for him at the office all the way up to seven o'clock this evening, and after that an important dinner with another valuable client. He sat back in his chair and swept his fingers through his hair, the floppily perfect dark blond strands falling back at an unconsciously rakish angle.

'Perhaps I should introduce her? Then no doubt all will become clear.' Getting to his feet, Oliver walked across to a door situated a few feet behind his desk and opened it. 'It's all right, darling…you can come in now,' he invited warmly.

The frown that was already furrowing Nash's perplexed brow deepened. He hardly knew what to expect before the slender dark-eyed brunette walked in. When she did, immediately he felt adrenalin pump through his insides, as though he was on a white-knuckle fairground ride. Although her exotic features were touched with just a mere application of make-up, and the plain dark grey suit she wore over a red wool sweater was not an outfit that was designed to demand attention, the face before him was immediately familiar. Freya Carpenter—an actress whose star had definitely been on the rise up until a couple of years ago, when there had been untold speculation in the press about her volatile marriage and her addiction to drink and possibly drugs.

Nash had met her once, at some celebrity bash he'd gone to, and although she'd looked more than sober enough at the time he'd been struck by how remote she'd appeared amidst the sea of well-known faces—as though the entire experience was an ordeal she'd really like to escape from. No…at that particular event it had been Freya's husband who'd been drinking too much and generally making a damn nuisance of himself. Nash remembered musing on how such a talented, beautiful girl could end up with such a loser. But if the rumours about her drinking and drug using were true, then clearly the woman's capacity for making good choices as far as her personal life was concerned was very definitely flawed.

Now, as he got to his feet and offered her his hand in greeting, of course he instantly knew why she might be in need of his help. Apart from the damage done to her reputation by accusations of drinking and drug-taking, two years ago Freya had also gone through the most horrendous divorce—an event that had been nothing less than trial by the media, and which had consequently lost her an important part in a major film because the producers had commented at the time that she was unstable. Then, just over a year ago, she had reportedly almost got herself killed in a car smash. Her ex-husband had very vocally reinforced the public perception that she'd been high on drink and drugs at the time. She'd been supposedly mourning their split, and the fact that he had left her for some nineteen-year-old fashion model who was pregnant with his baby.

Reading between the lines, and recalling her solemn face at that party whilst her husband had commanded most of the attention with his loud-mouthed antics, Nash now came to the conclusion that there was a hell of a lot more behind that story than the public had been led to believe. The young woman standing before him might have gone off the rails in her personal life, but she was still an actress with some highly notable roles to her name. She'd even graced the London stage a couple of times, and won critical praise bar none, so she was no bimbo just in it for the fame. That made it even more puzzling that she had wound up with a disaster like James Frazier.

The most recent slur to suddenly reignite frenzied interest in the actress had been speculation about her mental stability, and it had had the press camping out in droves on her doorstep for the past week. The story went that Freya Carpenter was all washed up: she'd suffered a major breakdown and was not likely to return to the stage or screen any time soon. Yes…it was obvious to Nash why Oliver Beaumarche's famous niece might urgently need the help of a man like him…

'Freya, this is Nash Taylor-Grant,' Oliver introduced her.

Warily, it seemed, she placed her chilled palm in his, and Nash saw her flinch as if contact with another human being—any human being—was tantamount to putting her hand into a tank of piranhas. Vaguely troubled, he volunteered a smile nonetheless. 'We've met before, Ms Carpenter…a long time ago at a party. I doubt that you'd remember.'

'I thought you looked familiar…although I have to say I can't recall the particular party.' Quickly withdrawing her hand, she pulled her glance away with it and went to sit in the seat that her uncle had positioned for her near his, her quick, light movements naturally graceful.

Once the men had resumed their seats, Oliver Beaumarche glanced very seriously at Nash. 'You will now have some idea as to why we need your help. I never told you about my connection with Freya before because naturally, as someone who cares very deeply about her welfare, my need to protect her privacy has always been paramount,' he commented, stealing a moment to smile at the reserved brunette. 'But now Freya wants to start rebuilding her career after the trauma she has been through, and she cannot do so unhindered while her unscrupulous ex-husband is still busy doing his utmost to undo every bit of good that she is trying so hard to achieve. Look at what has happened now, for instance! She has been nothing less than a prisoner in her own home after all this ridiculous nonsense in the press about her state of mind, and I do not doubt for a minute that the rumours were started by that good-for-nothing, unspeakable—'

'Please don't think that I am totally blaming my ex-husband for my recent lack of success, Mr Taylor-Grant,' Freya interjected quietly and her mesmerising, slightly smoky voice had the disarming effect of making all the hairs on the back of Nash's neck stand on end. 'I take full responsibility for what's happening in my life. It's my uncle who seems to believe that my reputation needs some help—though if you ask me after this latest fiasco I think it would probably be better if I just go quietly away somewhere and disappear until everybody forgets about me.'

An ironic little smile touched a mouth that was undeniably tinged with sadness yet still suggested the most riveting sensuality. As though hypnotised, Nash felt his gaze magnetised by it. He shifted ever so slightly in his seat. 'I don't think anyone who has read the papers or heard the news in the past couple of years would deny that your reputation has definitely taken a bit of a battering, Ms Carpenter. Nonetheless…I'm certain that there must be a lot of public sympathy out there for your predicament.'

A shadow of distress seemed to pass across her arresting features. Her slender shoulders stiffened beneath her unremarkable fitted jacket and her velvety brown eyes stared almost accusingly at Nash. 'I'm not looking for sympathy, Mr Taylor-Grant! And I'm not mentally unstable either! I'm angry, but then I think I have a right to be! Look…all I want is to be able to get on with my life again without interference. Can you imagine what it's been like being literally hounded by a pack of story-hungry reporters and photographers? If I did have a breakdown, could anybody blame me?'

'I don't think they could. It can't be pleasant,' Nash concurred.

'Besides…why should the public have sympathy for someone they believe had everything and then threw it all away because she let her private life go to rack and ruin? They probably think I got exactly what I deserved!'

'I'd hardly call a major car accident and defamation of character by someone I presume must have loved you once upon a time something that you "deserved"…. Would you?'

His words were like a cutlass, slicing her in half, and for a long, dreadful moment Freya was frozen by the wave of pain that throbbed sharply through her. Did he but know it, he was wrong about James loving her. Oh, his passionate words and declarations of being crazy in love with her had definitely convinced Freya that he was in earnest at the time, but she had quickly discovered that lies and deceit came very easily to him—especially when employed to get him whatever it was that would serve his own greedy ambition. But still Freya had to silently admit that she'd been complicit in all too easily believing his lies…

'Freya?' Her uncle's unfailingly kind eyes regarded her with more concern than she could handle right then. He'd been so good to her…so patient. And she wished that not even one single ounce of her predicament had ever visited its pain upon his heart.

'I'm fine…really. But if I'm honest…' She glanced at Nash and made herself endure the unflinching examination in his piercing blue gaze—an examination that seemed to reach deep inside her and see her soul laid bare… Was he looking to gain some advantage? she wondered. She'd learned the hard way to be wary in a profession that raised you up to the skies one minute and then sent you crashing back down to earth onto a bed of red-hot nails the next. Her uncle was too trusting for his own good sometimes. How long had he known this PR guru, anyway? Not long, was her guess. Though it was perfectly true that she remembered seeing Nash before…even though her comment about forgetting which party they'd met at had probably convinced him that she was probably too drunk or high at the time to remember.

Freya had been neither, and a flash of anger and despair assailed her. But, recalling the encounter with Nash, she remembered she'd certainly observed at the time that the man possessed an almost careless kind of male beauty and a sexual aura that was magnetising. She also recalled that the lissom beauty who had accompanied him that night had poured herself into the kind of tight-fitting dress that had made Freya wonder how she even breathed in it, let alone moved! The woman had spent practically the entire evening gazing up at her escort adoringly, as if there was no other man in the room but him.

It had been painful for Freya to witness such obvious adoration when her less than charming husband had been busy making a spectacle of both himself and her. Now, regarding Nash as he sat opposite her on the other side of Oliver Beaumarche's generous-sized desk, she guessed it would be all too easy to succumb to that frank, inviting demeanour of his and tell him everything…all the sordid little secrets of her disastrous soul-destroying marriage and the quite staggering mistakes she'd made along the way. The very thought was apt to make her doubly wary of the power he might so easily wield should she confess anything to him.

'I think this is a waste of time,' she continued. 'I'm in no hurry to get back into the limelight, Mr Taylor-Grant. I'm not saying I would never want to work in the industry again, but when I do it will definitely be behind the scenes. I've had my fifteen minutes of fame, and quite frankly I'd rather jump off a cliff than willingly submit my private life to the kind of vicious intrusion that I've had to endure ever again!'

'If you don't mind my saying so, Ms Carpenter, that's going to be a tall order under the circumstances.'

'How do you mean?'

'Well…' Nash crossed his legs at the knee of his dark

blue Armani suit, and rested his arms alongside the chair's dark cherry surround. 'So long as the press and the public keep speculating about you, and so long as your ex-husband keeps feeding them lies…I presume that they *are* lies?…then I doubt if you'll be allowed to get on with your life in peace and work behind the scenes as you desire. Have you even made a statement refuting your ex's most recent allegation?' he asked her. 'Not the one about you having a breakdown…the other one.'

Freya knew immediately what Nash was referring to, and she sensed heat rise in her face as his unwavering gaze locked onto hers with even more acuity than before.

'You mean that recent little slur about my sexuality? Do you think anyone really believes such salacious drivel?'

Nash said nothing. Although Freya's cheeks had turned slightly pink, he guessed it was more out of rage than embarrassment. Good for her! he thought privately. If she still had some fight in her after what her apparently malicious ex-husband had done to her then that would be all to the good in helping her work towards full recovery. Although if he was honest Nash still couldn't understand why she had given a waste of space like Frazier so much power over her life and her career in the first place. How people fooled themselves when it came to relationships. They took more care, it seemed, in choosing a car or a house than a life partner!

Determined to try and put his judgement aside— even though he privately thought she must have brought a lot of her disasters upon herself—Nash had no doubt that he could help Freya rebuild her career. He'd taken on many almost ruined reputations of people in the public eye before this, and helped restore them to a much more positive aspect. But if he accepted this job it would definitely be on the proviso that from now on her behaviour had to be far more exemplary than it might have been in the past.

'Well, I'm sure you don't need a lesson from me about people being easily manipulated by the media to believe almost anything they're told.' The broad shoulders beneath his beautifully tailored jacket lifted in a shrug. 'It's my view that you need to put an end to the publication of this "salacious drivel", as you so rightly referred to it. And to do that you need to lend the proceedings a little dignity, by making a very calm but firm statement refuting every defamatory remark that's been made by your ex.'

'Nash is right, Freya.' Oliver slid his big hand over hers and squeezed it. 'That man has got away with murder, and it simply can't be allowed to continue! If you cannot bring yourself to do something about this for yourself, then think about what your poor mother has gone through in all of this!' He directed his suddenly emotional gaze towards Nash and Oliver's dark eyes glittered. 'My sister has all but suffered a nervous breakdown because of what has gone on,' he explained. 'Where's the justice in that? James Frazier has no morals, and no remorse for anything he has done to our family, and he continues to carry on unchecked by anybody! Even the press is on his side! And even though he's maligned Freya's reputation, and all but bled her dry financially because of his lies in court—and because a well-known newspaper readily supplied him with some cutthroat lawyer from America, wanting to make a name for himself in the divorce—he still continues to cause havoc!'

The room seemed to spin a little. Freya was fine when she wasn't thinking about the devastating, almost unbelievable chain of events that had dragged her remorselessly down into the pits of hell, but hearing it stated out loud by her uncle, and registering the affecting passion in his voice, she wanted to find a remote desert island somewhere and remain there, forgotten by everybody until she died…

Why had she been so blind to the truth about James's character? she asked herself again in silent anguish. Why had she allowed herself to be so easily seduced by his lies? But again she had to consider that her downfall wasn't just due to her ex's bad behaviour. Some of the blame, if blame was to be apportioned, *had* to lie with her. Maybe if she hadn't fooled herself so convincingly that his regard was sincere because of her own desperate underlying need to be loved then none of this awful mess would have happened?

'Well…' Clearing his throat, and easing his striped silk tie away from his collar a little, Nash glanced briefly down at his watch. 'It seems to me, my friend, that only your niece can make the decision about what she wants to do. If you want me to help you, Ms Carpenter, then I will. But I will also need you to comply with how I suggest we proceed—to the letter.' Turning his gaze to Freya, he registered the stark unhappiness exposed to him in her coffee-dark eyes, and a genuine bolt of sympathy rippled through him. Lousy choices or no, she must have gone through hell, he thought. She was still going through hell, by the look of her…despite her initial insistence that she didn't need any help. 'Ms Carpenter?'

'This statement that you suggest I make…would you be willing to help me make it?'

There was the smallest flash of uncertainty in her dark-eyed glance, and Nash straightened in his chair. Satisfaction at the knowledge that she was going to relent to receiving some help pulsed through him, as well as gratification that he could do something to repay the generous friendship that her uncle had extended to him.

'Of course. If you decide to hire me to work on your behalf, Ms Carpenter, I can promise you that I will bring every ounce of expertise and assistance to your aid that is at my disposal.'

'Then I'll do it.'

Putting her hand up to her hair, she tucked a few silky strands behind her ear and looked as solemn as she had during that party where Nash had first met her. If he was any judge, right now she seemed to be garnering every ounce of steel she had left in her to face whatever was coming next—yet he also acknowledged that she must be dreading deliberately putting her life back under public scrutiny again.

In the absence of any further speech from his niece, Oliver leant across the desk and shook Nash's hand. 'Thank you, my friend. I have only known you for a short time, but I believe you to be a man of integrity and honour. Freya needs somebody like you on her side at long last… This dreadful situation has all but broken her.'

'What are you saying, Uncle Oliver? You know that isn't true!' Getting to her feet, Freya glared first at Oliver, then more pointedly at Nash. 'One thing I'd like to make very clear at the outset, Mr Taylor-Grant: I may have suffered a serious setback or two during the past couple of years—one or two broken bones in a car accident being the least of them, funnily enough—but I am not under any circumstances "broken". And even if I were…I'm not looking for anyone to "fix" me. I'm tougher than I look, and if I've survived what I've come through so far without going completely insane, then I'm quite capable of surviving more of the same without turning into some kind of pathetic jibbering wreck!'

'Well…it's my hope, and your uncle's too, I'm sure, that you won't have to endure too much stress and strain much longer, Ms Carpenter. Once you've made your statement to the press, we'll quickly get on with the task of helping you re-establish your career and getting you some very positive publicity for a change, so that you can do just that.'

The man in front of her appeared so utterly convinced

of what he was saying that something inside Freya—some frozen little shard—seemed to break away from the ice floe around her heart and suddenly start to melt in the first hopeful feeling she'd had in a very long time. When her uncle had first mooted the suggestion of seeing this friend of his, who was a big name in PR, she had been understandably reticent, uncertain that it would achieve anything good. But now, having properly met Nash Taylor-Grant, and in spite of her fear of ever placing her trust in a man again…any man…she felt there was something about him that suggested the kind of rock-solid strength and reliability that anyone in trouble would welcome. Something that told her he could negotiate a minefield on his wits alone if he had to, and get to the other side intact. And it wasn't just the sharp, elegant cut of his designer suit on a body that suggested he was a man in his prime in every way, or the defiant hardness of his jaw that threw out a challenge to 'do your worst' that convinced her. No…it was something innate in the man himself.

Having found her ability to trust severely battered after what James had done, Freya more than longed for her assumption about Nash to be true. But she'd lost faith in her judgement too…she couldn't deny that.

Sitting back in her chair, she smoothed her hand down the side of her skirt and tried to hold onto some of the previous hope she'd allowed herself to feel. When she raised her gaze to re-examine Nash's strongly handsome face, the blue of his eyes seemed to increase their potent wattage, and astonishingly Freya experienced a little dart of sensual awareness implode quietly yet devastatingly inside her.

'If you could really accomplish all of that…' She shrugged her shoulders a little, suddenly alarmed at the idea that he knew what that frank gaze of his had briefly done to her. 'I'd be in your debt, Mr Taylor-Grant.'

'Why don't you call me Nash? If we're going to be working together for a while formality only gets in the way…don't you agree?'

CHAPTER TWO

NASH cancelled his next two appointments and went back to the office to do his homework. He needed to act quickly if they were going to turn the tide of public consciousness in Freya Carpenter's favour, and, frankly, her loud-mouthed ex had had things his way for far too long. It was time to redress the balance. Having seen some of the evidence of the fine work that the actress was capable of, Nash was of the opinion that it would be a crying shame were she never to act in front of an audience again. And, being a friend of her uncle's, he felt a certain obligation to double his efforts in helping her. But to say that he'd been surprised by the revelation that Freya Carpenter was Oliver Beaumarche's niece was akin to being surprised to discover that the restaurateur was closely related to royalty! Not that Nash was impressed…it was just that it had come as the most unexpected shock. He'd known Oliver for a while now, and never at any time had the older man indicated that he had a famous niece. Or that she was a famous niece in deep trouble…

Tapping the end of his pen against his teeth, he leaned forward in his chair to more closely examine the glossy colour print that lay in front of him on the desk. He wasn't immune to the power of the darkly melting eyes that gazed back at him. Having seen them at close quarters for himself, he could see how a man would be apt to lose his sense of perspective if he looked into them too deeply and for too long… Their distinctly exotic slant helped to make them damn near unforgettable too. And when they were magnified up there on the big screen, as they had been in the past, would anyone be immune to their arresting impact?

Although in the picture before him her lips were parted in a smile, there was a vulnerability that lingered there too…a sensitivity that only the most hardened individual would be blind to. There were faces and people that scarcely left an impression…Freya Carpenter was definitely not one of those. With that amazing fall of rippling dark hair, as well as the slender, long-legged figure that she'd hidden almost primly behind that understated grey suit, her looks would guarantee her plenty of attention whether she was famous or not. A woman with that kind of stand-out sensual cachet could reel the men in like the most willing fish you ever saw… In light of that fact, Freya had certainly been unlucky in settling on a poor specimen like James Frazier to get hitched to.

Almost reluctantly setting aside the photograph, because its subject was frankly beginning to mesmerise him, Nash turned his attention to several different accounts of her headline-catching divorce, as well as the latest press speculation splashed all over the celebrity gossip pages, and he read them more carefully and avidly than a scientist reading the results of the most compulsive research…

The room had turned cold, and outside a fine drizzly rain was falling. Really, Freya didn't care one way or the other. Why should she care when the sky had already fallen in on top of her? The afternoon light was fading but, huddled into one of the deep corners of her once luxurious Fortnum and Mason sofa, she couldn't bring herself to move and switch on a lamp. Instead, she drew her legs towards her beneath the long wraparound skirt she wore with a baggy sweater and wrapped her chilled arms around her knees. It was definitely a 'hide under the duvet' kind of mood that had enveloped her, but she was too weary even to try and accomplish even that. She'd been endeavouring to read a long-time favourite novel—a kind of security blanket she reached for when times were tough and she needed to feel safe—but the words were a waving sea of hard-to-pin-down sentences, because her mind was too preoccupied.

What if she'd done completely the wrong thing in agreeing to make the statement Nash had suggested she make to the press? What if it just drew to her even more horrible and unwanted attention? Even now there were two or three photographers lurking around near her house, hoping to catch a glimpse of her. She could spot them a mile away! Returning to the idea of making a public statement, Freya groaned out loud at the prospect. What if her words came out wrong? Or she stumbled and they immediately concluded that she was indeed the 'wreck' that James had all but convinced them she was? A once bright star whose light had blazed all too briefly but had soon burned itself out, relegating her to the ranks of has-been.

Dropping her head into her lap, she squeezed her eyes shut tight and willed the world to go away. But, no matter how much she wished it, it never did. It was still there, in all the same washed-out colours, whenever she opened her eyes again. Her uncle was only trying to help her. She knew that. He believed in her talent even if the rest of the world didn't. He wanted her to work again, to express the gifts that he judged God to have blessed her with. But, in spite of her brave words in his office yesterday, when she had declared to Nash that she wasn't broken and that he shouldn't try to fix her, today was a different story. Today the twin demons of fear and self-pity had returned with a vengeance, like honed daggers attacking her in the dark, and all Freya wanted to do was hide.

The sound of the doorbell echoing through the house sent shockwaves flooding through her whole being and, lifting her head, she pushed back her hair from her whitened face. Uncurling her legs, she was almost disorientated by the primal river of panic that assailed her as she got shakily to her feet. The cold in the room and in her heart made her shiver almost violently. The only people who could possibly be visiting her legitimately would be her uncle or her mother—she didn't have an agent or a manager anymore, and most of her 'friends' had been conspicuous by their absence since her very public fall from grace. But both those two always rang her first, to warn her that they were coming.

Terrified in case the visitor was another mercenary reporter or photographer, taking the opportunity to catch her unawares—it had happened too regularly to be beyond a joke—Freya cautiously negotiated the crimson-carpeted corridor of the hallway in her bare feet, narrowing her gaze at the broad-shouldered shadow that hovered behind the opaque glass panels in the door. She froze for a moment, immobilised by fear. When she did finally move she hurried back inside the living room and, edging cautiously towards the large bay window, carefully moved aside a small section of the roll-down blind to peer outside.

The figure she saw standing on the wide front steps, his rain-dampened gilded hair a notable contrast against the expensive black cashmere of his overcoat, made her heart jump into her mouth. Nash! Her uncle must have trusted him enough to give him her home address, she guessed, but why hadn't he rung to warn her first?

Dropping the blind abruptly into place again, as though

it had suddenly turned into something unpleasant to touch, she smoothed her hands nervously down the sides of her rumpled skirt. Trying to banish the feeling of terror that gripped her at the thought of speaking to anyone today, she exhaled a long breath that was infused with both a kind of desperation and a sense of hopelessness. Dear God! Was she destined to spend the rest of her life hiding away from the rest of the world inside her own home? A home was meant to be a place of refuge…not a prison!

Her mouth feeling as dry as sawdust, Freya speared her fingers through her waving dark hair and reached a decision. She had no choice but to talk to him. After agreeing to make the statement yesterday, she couldn't now tell him that she'd changed her mind. There was always the danger that this man would also believe she was too unstable to be trusted if she told him to go away.

Reluctantly opening the door, she wrapped her arms across the beige coloured sweater that all but swamped her slender frame and briefly, jumpily, met the searing blue beam of Nash's immediately searching gaze.

'You didn't ring me to let me know to expect you,' she snapped accusingly. Although her words gave the impression that she was the one in charge of the situation, Freya's courage all but deserted her as she glanced up into her visitor's compelling visage.

'Yeah…I'm sorry about that.' He grimaced, but didn't appear overly concerned. 'Your uncle gave me your number, but I was nearby when he rang me in the car just now and I thought I wouldn't waste any time. I need you to fill me in on a few things, and I thought we could work on your statement together. Can I come in?'

Unable to think of an excuse in the world to deny him, Freya pressed herself back against the wall to let him pass her, then hurriedly closed the door again, her dark eyes making a swift reconnaissance of the street outside just before she did so, in case anyone should be taking a particular interest in her or her visitor. But, divertingly, the disturbing soft musk scent of Nash's masculine cologne impacted the air around her with unexpected sensuality, and she felt its potent effect immediately in the pit of her stomach and in her too-dry mouth. She told herself her reaction was simply down to nerves. All her responses were heightened by anxiety today, and she'd sell her last possession to access some calm from somewhere.

'Let's go into the living room.' Freya eased past him, making as much space between them as possible, before turning into the room she had so recently and reluctantly vacated.

Following her slender form, and wondering why she'd chosen to conceal it in clothes that seemed far too big, Nash was vaguely alarmed by the smudged mauve shadows he'd glimpsed beneath her fascinating eyes. Once inside the room he had another cause for alarm. There was a biting chill in the air that almost matched the freezing temperature outside. There was no evidence of heat at all, even though it was such a raw day. None of the several lamps that he could see around the room were turned on either, even though the evening's shadows were threatening the pale afternoon light that remained. The furniture seemed sparse, and apart from the plush cinnamon-coloured sofa dominating the centre of the room, and a matching high-backed armchair with a scarlet cushion, there were very few comforts that he could detect. A further disturbing bolt of concern shot through him.

'Aren't you cold?' he asked, before he could check the words. Freya regarded him as though his voice had just aroused her from the deepest of drugging sleeps. A little frown appeared in the softly pale space between her brows. 'I'm fine… But if you're cold, I'll switch on the fire.'

Before Nash could tell her it didn't matter, she had crossed the room and switched on a modern electric fire with fake coals in front of the old-fashioned fireplace. In just a second the gas burners burst into warm life, and he was glad for her sake that she had agreed to inject a little heat into the icy room. The woman looked as if she needed warming up in every way imaginable. Was this how she spent her days now that she'd retreated into near obscurity? he wondered. Alone in a big empty house in near freezing temperatures?

The thought was apt to make him want to throttle her ex-husband if this was what his mercenary deeds had reduced her to. He'd been reading quite a lot about James Frazier, and none of it did the man credit. On a scale of one to ten, in Nash's book the man had to score zero. As well as having sullied Freya's name as frequently as possible—both before, during and after their divorce—he had apparently been spending money like it was going out of style—money that, as far as Nash could ascertain, had come from the huge divorce settlement he'd won. And Freya had not retaliated either in word or deed. Not at any point.

He could scarcely understand it. What kind of legal advice had she been given? Why had her defence been so inept, and why had the courts decided in her husband's favour? Did he have some kind of hold over her? Nash had also learned that after their divorce Frazier had apparently invested huge amounts of money in unsound business deals that had more often than not backfired on him, losing him vast sums. But that hadn't curtailed his expensive lifestyle, it seemed. Having made some discreet enquiries late last night, and followed them up early this morning, Nash had discovered that Freya's ex was just about to leave for the Caribbean with his young blonde girlfriend and their baby, and he knew that it was time Freya made her statement and let the world hear her side of the story. After that, she could start to pick up the pieces and get her life and her self-respect back.

'How about turning on a lamp or two as well?' Nash suggested, keeping his voice low and friendly. As she seemed momentarily frozen into inaction he took the task upon himself. He moved towards the tall, fringed standard lamp by the window, and then over to another one situated on the opposite side of the room. Switching them on, he saw they made an immediate impact. With the fake fire now glowing, and the light from the lamps introducing a more amicable intimacy, Nash hoped that Freya might start to relax a little. He knew instinctively, even without regarding her worried features, that this whole business was going to be another huge trial for her, and he would have spared her any pain it might cause if he could. But he told himself that it was ultimately for her own good that they were doing this. The woman couldn't spend the rest of her days cloistered away like a nun who had taken a vow of silence.

'I'm a little rusty when it comes to entertaining visitors…I'm sorry. I should have offered you something to drink. I have some fruit juice—or perhaps you'd prefer some tea or coffee?'

'Why don't you just sit down and we'll talk?' Nash answered.

'Okay.' Clearly reluctant, as though his words had unhappily thwarted her instinct to escape into another room and get away from him, Freya resumed her seat on the couch. Taking off his overcoat, Nash sat down at the other end and stood his hide briefcase on the floor by his feet.

'So…what have you been doing today?' he asked interestedly. She blinked, appearing nonplussed for a moment—as though her brain could hardly compute the question, never mind find an answer.

'What do you think I've been doing?' she retorted, clearly annoyed. 'I'm under siege here…my whole life is under siege!'

'Then I guess the press have been making their presence felt in one way or another again? Well… tomorrow you'll get your chance to redress the balance and tell everyone the truth about things.'

'And do you think for one minute that they'll print the truth? You don't think that they might—just might— bend it a little, to suit whatever slant they've decided to take on that day?'

It was easy to understand why she was so angry. Nash would be too if it was his life that strangers were taking up a position on, manipulating information to sell newspapers. But then he hadn't entered a profession where fame was the currency that everyone secretly hoped for.

'I wonder that you want anything to do with the media…they're a bunch of vultures!' she added with feeling.

'You can't be blind to the fact that many artists and celebrities court the media? How else would they get their work promoted? Do you think film companies are in the business of making films to distribute to the public for free?' Shaking his head, Nash held her gaze with definite authority. 'What you've got to do is learn to play the media at their own game. Right up until now you've been the one that's clearly been wronged by your ex— and them—so the time is ripe to turn things around. The

British public in particular love an underdog. I'm sorry, Freya, but that's how you have to see it. After you've made your statement tomorrow, telling them your side of the story and refuting Frazier's slanderous allegations, you'll have everybody on your side again and that can't fail to attract more positive attention to help your career. Isn't that what you want?'

'I don't know…yes…I suppose.'

Her fingers intertwined and opened again several times as she said this, and Nash frowned at the sight. Never had a pair of slender hands appeared so pale and cold…almost as though they'd been dipped in ivory. He had the strongest urge to pull her into his arms so that he could hold her. He would have done it too, if he hadn't already known that to do so would probably propel him out of her life for ever. He owed it to Oliver, at least, not to risk such an outcome.

'All right, then… So, if I'm going to help you, I'll need your co-operation and not your hindrance. Don't think I don't understand your reluctance about appearing before the press again, because I do. This won't be easy, and I won't lie to you about that. But apart from what we have to do tomorrow there will be other things I need you to comply with…places I need you to appear, events I need you to attend…all in the name of achieving some positive publicity. And if you're reluctant to oblige then I can't do the job your uncle has asked me to do to help you…do you understand?'

There was a steely undertone to his calmly voiced reply, and Freya sensed that the man took great pride in seeing an assignment through and accomplishing it to the high standards that he no doubt exacted from himself and others. He did not appear to be someone who would let anything stand in the way of achieving that…no matter who they were. She told herself she should be pleased that he was prepared to be so diligent on her behalf, but right then—feeling the way she did—it was hard to be reassured by anything much. All she knew was that she was going to have to face the increased scrutiny of cameras and questions again, and her whole being baulked violently at the very thought—even though it was an exercise to help repair her damaged reputation.

Ceasing her fidgeting, Freya sat very still. Her expression was as calm as she could make it as she turned towards Nash.

'You say you understand my reluctance to appear before the press and the public again, but I wonder if you do?' Sighing, she swallowed hard before speaking. 'It's like a form of spiritual rape, you know? Like they can take everything from you and you can do nothing to protect yourself! Yes, I enjoyed my success when success came…but I never realised how essential my privacy was until all this happened. Should I be punished for that?' Stopping for a moment to glance towards the glowing fire, she brought her attention back to Nash again before speaking. 'Going through a marriage break-up is tough enough, without having to go through it in front of the media and the public. They all love you when your star is on the rise, but do you know how much they relish it when you start to wobble on that pedestal they've put you on?'

'You can't let anybody grind you down. You've just got to show them you're way too strong for that. Fight back, Freya! Don't let anyone relegate your existence to this house, this room, as if you're too afraid to live fully any more because you fear their judgement. That's just what they want you to do! Don't give them the satisfaction. Especially don't give your ex-husband the satisfaction of knowing that he's got some kind of hold over you.' His blue eyes narrowing, Nash compelled Freya to hear him out.

What he said struck an already very tender nerve. She'd fought James's lies up to a point, but after that he'd worn her down with his accusations and insults, and when his deliberate lying to the press about her had started to make some serious inroads into her self-esteem and personal confidence Freya had been too hurt and too mentally fatigued to fight him any more. Even in court she hadn't helped her own defence. Instead she'd blamed herself for everything that had happened...even told herself that she deserved it. She had the wonderful career she'd set out to achieve and now she had to pay. James Frazier was her nemesis.

'I have to ask this. Why didn't you sign a pre-nuptial agreement to prevent your ex from getting all your money? And why didn't you have a better lawyer to represent you? Surely your uncle could have—?'

Freya's hackles rose at that. Her almost translucent skin became very flushed. 'It's not my uncle's responsibility to do everything for me! I'm an adult…I make my own choices, even if they ultimately backfire on me! And as for a pre-nuptial agreement…' Her guilty glance was painful to witness. 'Suffice to say that James persuaded me that we didn't need one. I know you must think me the biggest fool that ever walked the planet, but what's done is done and I can't turn back the clock.'

'You say he "persuaded" you?'

Nash had honed in on that remark like an eagle swooping down on its far less swift prey, and Freya sensed the heat in her cheeks intensify. When that particular conversation had arisen between her and James it had ended with him throwing a frightening tantrum. He'd trashed her living room amidst threats of committing suicide, because she clearly didn't love him enough to trust him, and Freya had found herself trying to placate his wild distress by promising she would never bring the subject up again. Of course she'd been duped… She knew that now, to her everlasting shame.

'Did he hurt you?' Nash demanded.

'No…not physically. You'd be amazed at the creativity some humans can apply when it comes to inflicting pain. Anyway…what does it matter now? We both know how my marriage ended, and I can analyse where I went wrong until the cows come home, but it won't make the relationship any less of a catastrophe than it turned out to be!' she retorted defensively.

Was Nash judging her for marrying a man like James and not signing an agreement to protect herself financially? The idea that he was almost made her want to show him the door. Freya had had enough judgement from other people to last her a lifetime!

'The point is I've seen too many performers in your situation who have ultimately come to regret not signing a pre-nup,' Nash responded with a sigh, leaning forward and resting his elbows on his knees. 'Anyway, like you say, what's done is done…but if I'm going to help you I need to know that you're as committed to this enterprise as I am. I want to help you get your life back, but I want *you* to want that a hundred times more!'

'You have my word that I'll co-operate,' Freya replied softly, her dark eyes unable for a moment to hide the exquisite vulnerability that he'd witnessed in her photograph. 'I didn't lie to you yesterday, you know. I am tougher than I look. It's just that there are days when—there are days that I…'

'I know.' Nash knew what she meant, because he'd been there too. But that had been a long time ago when he'd been a very different person from the successful, confident man who sat here today. 'But the more you face the things you feel are impossible to face the stronger you'll become, Freya. Trust me…I know what I'm talking about.'

To Nash's intense relief, she dropped her shoulders

and stopped looking like a startled deer about to bolt. At some point in the not too distant future he was going to have to raise the thorny question of her alleged drinking and drug use… But he wouldn't hit her with that particular can of worms right now. Not that he didn't doubt she had great inner reserves… She might be feeling vulnerable, but he sensed strength there too. The woman couldn't have survived what she'd endured without it. A less strong person would have had a complete breakdown by now.

'Perhaps I will have a cup of coffee after all?' he suggested. 'Then we'll get to work on his statement.'

CHAPTER THREE

HE WAS getting ready to leave, and Freya found to her astonishment that she was strangely reluctant to see him go. For the first time in longer than she could remember she'd felt at ease in another human being's company, and she wanted to experience more of the same. As Nash's calm, almost hypnotic voice had drawn her out from behind the heavily guarded fence she'd erected between herself and the world she'd become afraid of returning to the morose mood that had afflicted her all day.

She didn't want to revisit that dark place. She'd lived in it for far too long and it was devouring her confidence. Already Nash had inspired her to want something different, something better. Listening to him read out the statement they'd prepared together, which she would read to the press tomorrow, she'd started to draw strength from the firmly assertive tone of the words. They made her sound in charge, not a victim any more. She was glad.

James had dictated how things would be for too long,

and her mistake in marrying him had been paid for a hundred times over—with too many tears, nearly all of her money, and a shattered career. This was where the tide started to turn. She wanted her life back. She wanted to be able to face people again and not shy away from them in case they judged or hurt her. She wanted to resume her career in some form or another that would give her satisfaction and help her support herself. And no longer would she foolishly pine for a love that was unconditional and lasting. Such a thing was as rare as orchids growing in the Arctic. It was simply futile and painful to even go there.

It stunned her that James seemed to hate her so much. Naively, Freya had believed that when he had won that huge settlement from her in the divorce it would be the end of his animosity and resentment towards her. But, no… The hints about her unstable state of mind, the vitriol with which he'd spoken of their 'dreadful and oppressive' marriage to all who would listen, the lies he had made up about her so-called addictions had all become worse. Freya was certain that the public's perception of her had been utterly poisoned by him. He'd painted her as a jealous bitch, an egotistical, demanding actress who constantly craved attention, when in fact the opposite was true. As a woman who was so insecure that she'd been jealous of every other woman James had looked at, especially if they were younger than her. Well, Freya was only twenty-eight years old herself…hardly over the hill!

The truth was that James had taunted her deliberately with his interest in other women to try and make her jealous. He'd hated his wife getting the attention, the adulation for her work that she'd eventually discovered he craved for himself. He'd never loved her. She wouldn't kid herself about that any more. He'd merely seen a chance to elevate himself by his association with her. An assistant cameraman when Freya had first met him, it had soon become evident that he had a driving ambition to be in front of the camera instead of behind it. She should have left him then, instead of agreeing to marry him.

When she looked back on what a gullible idiot she'd been, entering into such a disastrous relationship, Freya could hardly believe her own stupidity. The need for love, she'd discovered, could make sane people crazy. She might just as well have climbed into a barrel and thrown herself into Niagara Falls!

Reaching for his coat from the couch, Nash turned to Freya with a smile. There were two fascinating dimples in his hollowed-out cheeks when he employed that compelling gesture, and an intensely glowing heat seemed to inhabit her entire body as she gazed back at him. Because the points of her breasts had pinched shockingly inside her voluminous woollen sweater, she folded her arms protectively across her chest—as if Nash might see through the thick layers of clothing to the erotic reaction he had wrought underneath.

'One more thing before I leave,' he drawled.

'Yes?'

'What are you going to wear for this press inter-view tomorrow?'

'What am I going to *wear*?'

He considered her with the same kind of patience that a concerned adult might employ with a confused child.

'Whatever you decide, it has to be exactly right. Something plain, like that grey suit you wore yesterday, says "I want to hide". That isn't the image that we're trying to project, Freya. You want to show the world that you're done with hiding, as if you've got something to be ashamed of. Alternatively, something too glamorous might suggest false confidence… Do you see what I mean when I say it has to be just right?'

She did. 'I'll spend some time this evening choosing something suitable,' she promised.

Would Nash be shocked to see how sparse the contents of her wardrobe were? she wondered. She'd never had a stylist, or been an avid follower of fashion or anything, but she'd often been gifted glamorous clothing by eager designers wanting their designs promoted by a famous name. However, along with her antique furniture and jewellery, most of it had been sold to help meet the debts incurred by her court costs.

'Want me to come and take a look with you?' he offered.

Feeling sudden shame at her reduced straits, Freya lifted her chin even as her cheeks flooded with crimson.

'No, thanks. I know it might appear as though I've

let a lot of things slide, but I can assure you I'm still capable of picking out my own clothes!'

Her vehemence made Nash grin. It didn't hurt that his suggestion had piqued her pride. It demonstrated that she was still capable of displaying a little grit. Seeing the way she'd been when he'd first arrived—sitting alone in a freezing cold room without the light on—he had been concerned that depression had struck deep. Now he knew that it was only a low mood that had descended, and he was honestly relieved. It made him even more determined to help her return to the land of the living and claim the full life that was naturally hers.

'I've arranged for the press to meet you at my office, and I'll be here at about nine in the morning to pick you up and take you back there. I want to make everything as easy as I possibly can for you, and I don't want you veering off into fantasy land, imagining everything is going to be horrendous. I'll be right beside you, and you're going to be just fine,' he told her. 'Of that I have no doubt. When it's all over we'll spend some time talking about how it went. After that, I believe your uncle has arranged for us to have lunch with him at his restaurant.'

'He's always trying to feed me,' Freya quipped, with a little half-smile playing about her pale lips. 'He thinks I don't eat enough.'

'Do you?' Nash asked sharply.

'I don't look like I'm starving myself, do I?'

Nash let his gaze rove boldly down her body, in the

baggy sweater and floor-length skirt, and his blue eyes glinted with humour. 'How would I be able to tell in that outfit? Do you always cover up like that?'

Out of the blue a memory came to him of Freya playing the female lead in an action/adventure movie he'd seen about four years back. Her role had been that of a fiery slave-girl in a sultan's harem, and she'd been all long tanned legs and curves aplenty. Just the recollection alone helped Nash get hot under the collar.

'It's a cold day, and I was trying to keep warm,' she replied testily.

'Then put the fire on,' he advised, walking to the door. He turned to briefly face her again, his expression serious but not bereft of kindness. 'Try and get a good night's rest. You're going to need all the energy you can muster for tomorrow. If you need me for anything…anything at all…here's my number.' He handed her a small business card. 'Sleep well, Freya.' And with that he departed.

Unmoving for several minutes after he'd gone, Freya stared down at the little card in her hand as if it was the first lifeline she'd been handed in a long time. Nash might only be helping her because of her uncle's claim on his friendship, but she couldn't deny she was glad to have someone like him on her side. There was something about the man that told her he could handle almost anything…that nothing would faze him because he'd seen it all—both the light and the dark side of human existence. Now, what had brought on that belief?

Shivering, Freya headed determinedly for her bedroom. She needed to survey the somewhat diminished contents of her wardrobe and decide what she was going to wear during her big ordeal tomorrow, when she would voluntarily face the press after so long spent trying to avoid them…

Nash dropped into his office to check that everything was ready for the press visit before going to collect Freya the next morning. He'd hardly been able to sleep for reflecting on their meeting yesterday. She hadn't confirmed it in so many words, but the idea that she'd been living like a hermit for the past two years, with only her uncle and her mother to stand by her in the face of all that had happened, had elicited a fierce, almost physical protest inside him. Injustice of any kind was apt to raise his hackles like nothing else, and he never failed to be astounded at the base depths some human beings could sink to in order to exploit another. She was well rid of her grasping, loud-mouthed ex-husband, that was for sure, and the best revenge in his book was always success. Nash didn't doubt for a second that Freya's star would rise again once her confidence had returned—and return it would. He would make sure of that.

Raising a corner of the cream-coloured blind at the window, he glanced broodingly down at the gleaming black Mercedes with personalised number plates parked beside the kerb below. Then, turning his head, he considered the dozens of signed celebrity photographs that were displayed round his office walls. He felt the ease and luxury of the bespoke suit he wore, which perfectly complemented his strong, hard physique. His good fortune never ceased to gratify him. In the inauspicious beginnings he had had, dreams of the kind of amazing success Nash enjoyed now had been either delusions or fantasies in other people's book. Yet he had still dreamed, and he had turned his dream into a reality.

But the thought wasn't entirely benign. It immediately provoked a disturbed frown between his dark blond brows, and for a moment Nash was consumed by some of the darker memories of his past. He'd been at the top of his profession for nearly six years now, but it never failed to bring him back down to earth when he remembered the painful and arduous route that had got him there. The point was he had risen above his seemingly insurmountable difficulties and succeeded. Now he needed to show Freya that she could do the same.

In the privileged circles that he moved in Nash enjoyed an admirable reputation amongst peers and clients alike, and he'd no doubt been helped by a biography that boosted the credentials he already had...even if some liberties had been taken with the facts... Most people assumed that he came from a fairly privileged background, with professional people as parents, and had benefited from a top-class education at a British public school. After all, his enunciation was perfect, with no traces of a Swedish accent at all. But

Nash wasn't the best publicist in the country for nothing. He'd never resorted to out-and-out deceit—but he intimately understood people's tendency to put two and two together and make five and he knew how to use it to his advantage.

From very early on in his career he'd been able to get away with revealing very little information about his origins—just a half-truth here or there, helped along by allowing various untrue assumptions to go unchallenged. That being the state of play, eventually a story had built up around him that was now more or less accepted as fact. He was Nash Taylor-Grant, raised in Suffolk, England, by a Swedish mother who was a chemist and a British father—an eminent scientist who had unfortunately died from a heart attack abroad on a business trip. There was also some vague notion that following his school years Nash had naturally gone on to Oxford or Cambridge—or at least one of the country's other leading universities.

The reality could not have been starker...

He hadn't been raised in Britain at all. He had been raised in a poor suburb of Stockholm in Sweden, the only son of Inga Johannsson—a laboratory technician who'd been forced to give up her job when she fell pregnant with Nash and had eventually had to work as an office cleaner just to keep body and soul together for herself and her small son. Nash's father had in truth been British. Nathan Taylor had been a biologist at the same laboratory where Inga had worked, and that was how the two of them had met. Unfortunately, when Nash was only three years old, his father had been killed in a car accident. With no compensation because she'd been unmarried, and no family to whom she'd been able to turn for help, Inga had had to get by on welfare. There had followed a series of disastrous relationships with the kind of men who would easily have found a niche in horror movies.

Flinching now from possibly the worst memory of them all, the time he'd witnessed yet again his mother being verbally and physically abused, Nash couldn't help but shudder. He remembered lunging at the man— his mother's current lover—and pummelling him with blows so hard that he'd split and broken the skin on his bare knuckles. But that had been before the man had turned on Nash and, with his far superior weight and strength, all but beaten him to a pulp. It would have been bad enough if Nash's ordeal had ended there, but neither he nor his mother could have anticipated what had happened next. In one horrific, unexpected act his attacker had produced a flash of something silver from inside his jeans pocket and torn open Nash's flesh with a flick-knife.

He'd almost lost his life that night. He'd certainly lost a good deal of blood, and put the fear of God into his poor mother as she'd sat weeping and wailing beside him in the ambulance that had gone screaming through the streets to take him to hospital.

Shame, hurt and fury moved through Nash's body

in one relentless wave of white-hot emotion as he remembered. Somewhere at the side of his ribs the old wound throbbed with renewed pain, and for a moment or two he really struggled to regain his equilibrium. Moving restlessly away from the window, he picked up the file he'd started on Freya Carpenter to will away the distracting and painful recollections that were bombarding him.

Yes…he'd experienced first-hand how human beings could wilfully hurt and maim each other—whether physically or with words—and because of that he had a genuine ability to understand the kind of hell this woman must have had to endure. But although he knew deep down that he didn't deserve to feel shame about his past any more, there was a part of him that still couldn't allow himself to admit the truth to everyone. He wished he could get over his own mistrust and think to hell with it, but it wasn't proving easy. Only time would tell if he would ever be at ease with himself enough to adopt such an approach…

As the press and television cameras whirred away in the small courtyard of Nash's smart Belgravia offices, before Freya read out her statement, he moved his gaze from the blur of journalists and photographers gathered round to study the woman that was the centre of so much clamouring attention standing by his side.

Astonishing beauty like hers scarcely needed the adornment of fine clothes and cosmetics to enhance it, but Nash would be a liar if he didn't concede that the elegant pink Chanel suit she wore—along with the perfectly applied make-up—elevated her looks to the realms of stand-out gorgeous. He already knew that the camera loved her—he'd seen the results often enough in photographs and on film—but now he could intimately see why. But did anyone but him guess that beneath Freya's faultlessly applied make-up her skin had the same pale sheen as ice-cold ivory?

Even now he sensed her tremble, and he deliberately slid his arm loosely round her small waist and gave her a reassuring squeeze. At that moment he didn't much care how the gesture might be misinterpreted. All he knew was a genuine desire to let her know that she wasn't alone, that he was firmly in her corner and would be staying there for the duration.

She turned briefly to acknowledge him, and the glint of warmth in her dazzling dark eyes momentarily un-steadied him. Clearing his throat, Nash addressed the small crowd in the courtyard. 'Ms Carpenter will now read out her statement, after which I will allocate just five minutes for any questions. All she and I would ask is that you accord her due respect and politeness for the great courage it has taken her today to speak out after two years of dignified silence. Thank you.'

It was over, and Freya knew she was still alive because her heart was beating strongly in her chest and her taste-buds could easily distinguish the strong Italian flavour of the coffee that she was sipping. Now alone with Nash, sitting on the stylish sofa in his office, her glance taking in the celebrity photographs that adorned the walls—many of whom she'd met—she could almost attest to breathing normally again.

'First hurdle over,' he commented, reaching for his own coffee as he settled himself in the matching armchair opposite. 'How does it feel?'

'What do you think?' Grimacing, Freya crossed one long slim leg over the other and saw Nash's gaze gravitate there almost immediately. For a moment it distracted her to be the recipient of that brooding and arresting cynosure, and the words she'd been about to speak got temporarily lodged inside her throat. She coughed a little to cover her unease. 'I feel like I've done a fire-walk…only I don't have the elation flooding me that's supposedly the result of doing one of those! Instead I'm wondering what I've started and if anything I've said will make a difference. If you want me to be frank…I'm also concerned about how James will retaliate. What I said doesn't exactly put him in a good light.'

Her words made Nash sit up in his chair, his cup of coffee returned swiftly to the table in front of him. 'Has he threatened you in any way?' he demanded.

'Do you mean physically?' Freya answered quietly, looking pensive. 'No. He has a good enough command of the English language to do enough damage using words alone. If you've read any of the newspaper reports from the past two years you must have noticed that.'

'You cry wolf enough times in my experience and you're going to get a kickback. I think the public are already drawing their own conclusions as far as your vindictive ex-husband is concerned, Freya. People aren't fools… '

'Words can cut so deep. Sometimes I think they can pierce the skin far worse than any physical violence. They have a way of inflicting damage where you're most vulnerable. That was James's particular little trick, anyway.'

'Even so…you can fight back.'

'Fight fire with fire, you mean? That's not my way.'

'I meant by getting on with your life again…by being a success! If you give up your acting career because your ex made you feel so bad that you can't face the world then he's won, Freya! You've made your statement today, stating the true facts of the case, and I know there'll be a lot of sympathy out there in return for your candour. After this you're bound to be in demand for all kinds of interviews, and depending on who's organising them and what their agenda is I'd advise you to agree to some of them. But don't worry…I'll guide you on that. If it means more positive publicity, then that's ultimately what we want. Plus it would get you back into appearing before the public again, and it might also help you rebuild some confidence.'

'I'll have to think about it.'

Leaning more fully against the chair-back, Freya

looked reticent. Nash wasn't blind. He could see that the woman was hurting, and hurting badly. It was becoming evident to him that she had suffered greatly in the past two years, and right now it was probably hard for her to believe that anything good could ever happen to her again. For someone with all the amazing assets she had it was a crying shame. Still, Nash wasn't in the business of lost causes. He was in the business of putting reputations to rights again.

'Remember what we agreed yesterday?' he prompted her, leaning forward and resting his hands on his knees. 'You have to give this enterprise your all! And it's not as though you have to negotiate all the hurdles on your own. I'll be with you, backing you up all the way…that's a promise.'

'What if public reaction isn't good? What if people still believe everything James has said about me?'

'It won't happen. Public sympathy will be totally on your side, Freya. Trust me, I know this business intimately. After today they'll know the truth about Frazier at last, and any further interest will be because people want you to do well again. Anyone who saw you out there today could easily see that you were a million miles away from being on the verge of a breakdown. You looked and were…amazing.'

They were just words, and Freya knew that, but she didn't doubt in those few charged moments that Nash meant them. She was only human, and could she help it if they melted her a little? Made her want more of this man's honest regard? Yet, even so, she knew the regard she craved ultimately had to come from inside herself. She couldn't afford to make any more mistakes, or constantly search for validity outside. Such a useless endeavour was always going to put her in a weak position and ensure her continuing vulnerability.

'Thanks. The suit helped. Uncle Oliver bought it for me when I attended my first awards ceremony.' Uncrossing her legs, she leaned forward to place her cup on the polished wooden coffee table between herself and Nash. Her lips quivered a little as she tried to form a smile. She was anxious that he wouldn't think she was deliberately fishing for compliments.

'It's a nice suit,' he agreed, an enigmatic smile of his own alighting on his highly sensual mouth.

financially ruined her, and having then been driven to explain her actions publicly to defend herself…well, it had left her feeling a bit like an ant squashed by a heavy boot.

She lifted her gaze to observe the man sitting opposite her. Nash did not seem to be eating much of the delicious food that had been placed in front of him either. That inscrutable brow of his seemed to denote that he was thinking hard about something, and Freya wondered if he was considering that she should have made more of a stand against her ex-husband's vicious slander? To a man whose demeanour and presence suggested he was capable of dealing with any disaster— whether personal or public—it was probably beyond understanding that a person's self-esteem and will could be so crushed by someone far more manipulative and clever that they were, almost paralysed into inaction. Well, he was wrong if he thought her heart wasn't really in this battle, Freya considered with force. She knew it was time to fight back and put things right in her life. It was just taking a little time to acclimatise herself to the idea of voluntarily putting herself under the public gaze again—especially when her experience of it during the past two years had been so relentlessly negative.

'I've been thinking,' he said now, his deeply blue eyes focusing intently on Freya's face. 'It might be a good idea if we got you away from here for a few days. Interest is already hot after your statement today, and it's going to get even hotter. I've already received a couple of text messages from my secretary saying the phone hasn't stopped ringing since the interview. It might help to get a little relaxation and some sun in before we proceed with part two of our campaign. How does the South of France sound to you?'

'I've been telling her that she needs a holiday for the past two years!' Oliver exclaimed, animation lighting up his eyes—eyes the same silky brown as his beautiful niece's. 'But will she listen? I think it's a wonderful idea, Nash! Do you know of a place that's private, where she won't be disturbed?'

'I have a place of my own in the Dordogne,' the other man replied, his glance somewhat guarded as he moved it to the woman sitting beside Oliver...as though he were still carefully weighing up the suggestion in his mind. 'It's right in the heart of the countryside, and about twenty miles from the nearest town. We can go there.'

'We?' Freya stared at Nash in astonishment. Did he really mean them to go to the South of France together, and stay in a place that was miles from anywhere? She barely knew this man and he barely knew her! Did he really expect her to run pell-mell into the unknown with him without so much as a by-your-leave? Coiling her hair behind her ear, she let her dark eyes duel bravely with his now disturbingly dancing azure glance. It didn't help that he seemed to be mocking her a little. Did he think she'd back down and refuse to go because she was too scared of taking such a risk?

'It will be the perfect opportunity for me to get to

know you better, Freya. It's important that I learn as much about you as I can, since we're going to work together. And besides that it will get you out of the eye of the storm for a while. As well as being able to relax a bit more, without constant press intrusion, there'll be plenty of opportunity for being physically active too. There's some stunning countryside to walk in, as well as a pool at the house.'

The South of France sounded highly tempting, Freya had to admit. It conjured up lazy sun-drenched days, tempting culinary aromas, and the kind of relaxation that her body and mind craved deeply. Her uncle was right— she did need a holiday. Yet there was still the knotty little problem of going with Nash. Could she trust him as much as he seemed to be taking it for granted that she should? It was a tall order after what she'd endured at the hands of her ex-husband and a bloodthirsty press.

Silently acknowledging that she was too mentally fatigued to argue the case any more, Freya came to a decision. She would go. At the end of the day, Nash was a friend of her uncle's, and Oliver Beaumarche was no mean judge of character. The people he befriended usually became friends for life. And he wouldn't have even considered asking Nash to help if he thought the man was untrustworthy in any way.

She picked up her glass of mineral water and sipped it before replying. 'The thought of getting away from this circus is definitely appealing. When would we go? Don't you have to arrange things at work and at home?'

'I've got no one to answer to at home, as I live alone, and as things turn out I'm due some free time. Plus…this *is* work for me, remember?'

He smiled, and the smile highlighted the two fascinating thumbprints in his cheeks…dimples! Freya wished she didn't keep noticing things about him that distracted her from the matter in hand, but it wasn't easy when the man exuded an aura that would stun a room full of people into silence merely because he had entered it.

Yet what did it signify that Nash was a highly attractive man? She'd been around enough of them to know that the outside packaging meant very little, and it certainly didn't follow that she had to succumb to that attraction in any way. She didn't want to sign up for any more pain or shock, and she didn't want the rest of her life to be like the car crash she'd suffered a year ago. From now on Freya wanted to make good choices…wise choices that served her and didn't sabotage her efforts to improve her life. Nash had been hired to help her achieve some positive publicity and to rebuild her damaged reputation so that she wouldn't have to resume her career under a cloud. Other than that, their relationship would remain purely professional and platonic…she was absolutely certain about that.

'We'll leave the day after tomorrow, if that suits?' he suggested.

'Good,' Freya answered with unguarded frankness. 'The day after tomorrow is fine with me.'

Oliver beamed at them both.

* * *

'Hello?'

In her bedroom that same evening, Freya answered the ringing telephone, expecting her mother to be on the other end of the line. They'd talked earlier, after Freya had returned from lunch, but she often rang more than once in a day, to ascertain that her daughter was taking proper care of herself.

'You silly little bitch!'

It very definitely wasn't her mother. Instead, a harsh-sounding male voice ripped into her, sending icy chills charging violently down her spine. James. She dropped down onto the bed with its neatly spread satin eider-down, her heart racing.

'I've changed my number…how did you get it?'

'I have my contacts, as I'm sure you know. Anyway…what the hell do you think you're doing, rubbishing me in public like you did today? I warned you about making trouble for me, didn't I?'

Freya heard the resounding thud of her own heartbeat in her ears, despising the fact that her whole body was trembling as though she'd just emerged from a freezing plunge-pool. Yet, thinking of her new resolve to turn her life around, she knew that she couldn't keep on letting this cruel, manipulative man belittle or frighten her. She really did have to start fighting back.

'Leave me alone, James! We're over! Remember? You're nothing to do with me any more! And I didn't rubbish you to the press earlier today…I merely spoke the truth—something I should have done a long time ago. And if you try to get in touch with me again, or threaten me, then I won't hesitate to call the police and tell them what you're doing!'

'Do you really think they're going to believe you? Everyone knows you're a crazy, spoiled little bitch!'

'It's not me that's crazy, James.' It was hard to keep her voice steady, but deliberately drawing upon her acting skills Freya managed it. 'And if you make any more defamatory remarks like that, my lawyers will be contacting you too.'

'Who's helping you? Is it that meddling rich uncle of yours? Tell him from me to mind his own bloody business and keep his nose out of where it isn't wanted!'

'Why don't you tell him yourself? Or can't you do that because the truth is you're not so sure about coming out on top in that fight? You're only capable of threatening women! Why don't you just get on with your life and let me get on with mine? You've got your girlfriend and your baby and most of my money…surely that's enough to keep you from feeling so dissatisfied?'

'I won't be satisfied until your name is dirt—until people say "Freya Carpenter? You mean that crazy, no-talent actress? What ever happened to her?"'

He slammed down the phone in a temper, and Freya shakily returned the receiver to its rest and covered her face with her hands. 'Please, no… Not again.'

Minutes later, she almost catapulted up to the ceiling when the phone rang again. Feeling sick with nerves, she snatched up the receiver and said loudly, 'Right! As soon as I put down this phone I swear I'm going to ring the police!'

'Freya? What's happening? It's me…Nash.'

'Nash?' She almost crumpled with relief. Sliding her fingers through her long waving hair, she couldn't stop shaking. 'I'm sorry about that…I thought it was James.'

'Have you talked to him? Has he been round there?'

'No, he hasn't been round, thank God! He rang me just now. I thought today might spark off something with him. I knew he'd be mad at me for speaking out.'

'Are you okay?'

'I am now.'

'According to my information, he's supposed to be flying out to Antigua today. Did the call sound like it was long-distance?'

'It might have been. I don't know…I couldn't really say.'

'Obviously he threatened you? What did he say?'

There was such command in Nash's voice that Freya didn't think to play down the truth. Besides, it was a relief to be able to tell someone what was really happening for a change, instead of pretending things weren't so bad and bearing the situation on her own.

'He said he won't be satisfied until my name is dirt, and that he's warned me about making trouble for him… Do I have to go on?' she replied, her skin feeling clammy now that the shock was slowly ebbing away. Dragging the silky blue eiderdown onto her lap, she spread it over her knees.

Detecting the weariness in her tone, Nash clenched his granite jaw tight. After the guts it must have taken for her to speak out to the press earlier on today, it must have been like a kick in the teeth to receive a threatening late-night phone call from that bastard Frazier, he thought. Examining the cut-crystal glass that he'd half filled with brandy, he swirled the darkly golden liquid round a little before placing it down on the windowsill untouched.

'No, sweetheart,' he conceded a little huskily. 'You don't have to go on. What you've just told me illustrates the picture perfectly. You should have rung the police straight away…did you?'

'No. It hasn't helped me in the past, so why should it now? Every time I reported anything James always got to them straight after and told them I was making it all up because I was lonely or drunk or high, and I craved attention.'

'How the hell has he still got your number? Didn't you have it changed when all this kicked off?'

'Of course I did! More than once. But he said he has contacts—whatever that means. How he gets my number, I don't know.'

'Well, I have some contacts myself, at Scotland Yard, and rest assured I'll be talking to them as soon as I get off the line to you! How are you feeling now? Do you want me to come over?'

'I don't think he'll try ringing again… Anyway, I won't answer the phone any more tonight. I'll be fine.

I've been dealing with this sort of thing for a long time now…I should be used to it. You don't have to come over, but thanks all the same for offering.'

Nash had real trouble accepting her assertion. He knew first-hand what it was to witness a man's intimidation of a woman, and nothing could unleash his fury more than that. She probably wouldn't sleep, he told himself, thinking of her walking round that chilly house all alone. And after a night with no sleep she was going to have the added challenge of dealing with a barrage of reporters and photographers waiting for her on her front doorstep in the morning. As he'd told her earlier at lunch—interest would be hot after today's statement.

Staring out of the sixth-storey window of his Westminster apartment, he contemplated the London skyline in all its twinkling late-night glory. It was a privilege he enjoyed most nights, and he never took it for granted. For a boy who had been raised in a tiny flat in the backstreets of Stockholm, it was the difference between a palace and a hovel. Rubbing his hand round the back of his neck, Nash quickly revised his plan of going to Freya's in the early hours of the morning to give her some support with the press and came up with a far better idea.

'Pack a bag,' he ordered bluntly.

'What?'

'Get your passport, throw some things into a suitcase and get ready to leave. I'm coming over there to pick you up and bring you back to my place. You can stay here until we travel to France on Friday morning.'

'That's a little extreme, isn't it?'

'Extreme? After what you've just experienced? Listen to me, Freya… I won't take the chance of Frazier bothering you again tonight, and this is the best way to ensure that he can't get to you. You already know that tomorrow morning there's going to be even more media interest, and probably a crowd of photographers and reporters waiting to catch you leaving the house… That's if they aren't there already?'

'I've got about a half a dozen of them camped out on my doorstep.'

'That clinches it, then. I should have thought of it earlier, but you'll definitely be better off at my place.'

There was silence at the other end of the line. Feeling his skin prickle with an acute sense of foreboding, Nash made his voice sharp. He knew she must be feeling at a pretty low ebb after that phone call, and he didn't want to risk her getting any lower and doing herself some harm. If she'd been addicted to drugs it crossed his mind that they might have been prescription drugs. What if she had a drawer full of powerful sleeping pills, for instance? Perhaps she'd never consider such a thing in a million years, but Nash didn't know her well enough yet to easily dismiss the possibility.

'Freya? Did you hear what I just said?'

'I heard you,' she answered, that mesmerising brushed-velvet voice of hers making a whisper-soft imprint on the part of him that wasn't entirely impervi-ous to more tender feelings. 'This isn't normal, living like this…is it? I wonder if my life will ever be normal again? If I'll ever be able to have any peace?'

How often had Nash reflected on those very same thoughts when he'd been going through hell all those harsh years ago, when he'd lived in his hometown? Well, he had turned dark beginnings into a far brighter future, and so would Freya. Nash would show her how or die in the attempt! It was fast becoming clear to him that this woman could really benefit from some time away from the scene of all her unhappiness. Oliver had confided in him that his niece hadn't left the UK in almost two and a half years—apparently he'd tried to persuade her to take a break abroad many times, and the restaurateur had homes in Spain and New York she could stay at—but the mental cruelty that Frazier had visited on her had made her almost agoraphobic.

'You just need a change of scene, sweetheart. Going to France for a while will be good for you. Staying at home you've just got all the same things and associations that you face every day, and they're like permanent reminders of everything that seems wrong in your life. Leaving them behind for a while will help you see things in a new perspective.'

'You must think I've completely lost the plot—but I wasn't always like this.'

'I know, Freya. I've seen you up there on the silver screen, remember?'

'That was a long time ago. I was a very different girl then.'

'Not so very different.' Catching his reflection outlined in the huge plate-glass window that encompassed a stunning view of the Thames, Nash saw a brief flash of pain register on his face. He couldn't pretend her words had glanced off him without making a dent somewhere. 'Life's just knocked you about a bit... It will get better, I promise.'

'What makes you so sure?'

'Good instincts.' He grinned at his own sense of certainty. If only he could transfer some of it to the traumatised woman at the other end of the phone...

'Well, if you're so sure that staying at your place tonight and going to France is the right thing, then I'll go and pack my suitcase.'

He heard her sigh, but this time there was definite resolve in her much more steady voice and Nash was relieved. 'I'll be there in half an hour,' he promised, then rang off and straight away depressed the numbers on his cordless phone for Scotland Yard, thinking as he did so that an ordinary member of the public was probably accorded more protection from the law and from friends and family than this lovely, talented woman whose face had graced movie screens...

A faint misty light was coming through the slatted silk blinds, dappling the damson-coloured duvet on the bed, and, blinking her eyes open in surprise, Freya sat up in a flash, barely knowing where she was for a moment. Peering at the illuminated digits on the alarm clock on the cabinet beside her, she registered the time in amazement. Five past seven!

'I don't believe it!' she muttered, checking again. She'd slept right through the night without waking up once…something almost unheard of! She was shocked to her marrow, especially as she had been sleeping in a strange bed as well.

She glanced round the spacious, frighteningly neat room, with its definitely masculine décor—there was no hint of anything remotely feminine amongst the muted colours and expensive modern furniture that she could easily detect—and, drawing her knees up to her chest, wrapped her arms around them as she contemplated her situation. Last night she'd been too tired and mentally fatigued after the phone incident to enter into a protracted conversation with Nash about what had happened. As it was, her nerves had been even more frazzled by the clamour of photographers almost swamping her and Nash as he'd spirited her away from them to his waiting car.

On reaching his apartment, she'd declined the nightcap and alternative cup of tea he'd offered and asked if he would mind if she just turned in. Immediately he'd shown her into this bedroom, which was easily reminiscent of a suite at a top-class hotel, and told her to try and get a good night's rest. When he'd said the words Freya had hardly believed that such a thing was possible, but here she was, seven hours later, feeling more rested and more refreshed than she'd done in absolutely ages.

Was it the distinct feeling of security she'd received from knowing that she was in Nash's domain and effectively under his protection? Was that why she had slept so well? That late night call from James had shaken her up badly, and to be honest when Nash had mentioned her spending the night at his flat part of Freya had been utterly relieved that he'd suggested it. Should she now berate herself because her defences had been low and she'd accepted an offer of help? If she'd accepted more help during the past two years when she'd needed it, then maybe she wouldn't have ended up as mentally bruised and battered as she was.

Feeling suddenly guilty that Nash might be already up and about and starting his day while she was still in bed, Freya threw back the duvet and put her feet to the floor. Just as she did there was a soft knock at the door.

'Freya? Are you awake?'

'Yes…I was just about to get up. Come in.' She extended the invitation automatically, without thinking.

Pushing the door wide, Nash was hardly prepared for the sight of one very shapely brunette, scantily clad in a flimsy red silk camisole with spaghetti straps and—as far as he could tell—matching panties, sitting on the bed rubbing the sleep from her very seductive dark eyes while her glorious dark hair cascaded freely down over her shoulders. His blue eyes locked onto her startled gaze with undisguised heat, and he had to ruefully tear them away when, realising how she must appear, Freya grabbed the duvet and quickly covered her exposed lower half with it.

'I'm sorry! I should have grabbed my robe,' she muttered, clearly embarrassed.

'It's me that should apologise,' Nash drawled, helplessly admiring the sight of her again, and laying a hand against his chest in the pristine white shirt as if to somehow corral his suddenly thundering heartbeat. The corners of his mouth hitched upwards into a definitely roguish grin. 'Except that I feel I should be thanking you too.'

'Thanking me? What for?'

'What for?'

His blue eyes glittering like the most compelling sapphires, he shrugged in disbelief. 'Sweetheart, if you have to ask me that then you really *have* been leading a sheltered life for too long!' he teased.

CHAPTER FIVE

SHE hadn't been to France for years. The last time had been when she'd attended the Cannes Film Festival—not to promote a film she'd had a role in, but as moral support for a friend of hers who'd made a very engaging film short. They'd had a wonderful time, Freya recalled, reminiscing as Nash drove their hire car through deserted French country roads. She sat beside him, her eyes shielded behind the pair of obligatory black sunglasses to keep out the glare of the midday sun and also to hide behind should some opportunist paparazzi happen to spot her.

She had always intended to venture into the French countryside one day and see for herself the scenery and way of life that so many ex-pats were enthralled by, and Freya's gaze alighted on the gently lilting verdant landscape with a quiet yet discernible excitement blossoming inside her. If she had to give an opinion on what she'd seen so far she would say that rural France was like an elegant apple tartan while its English equivalent was more akin to a sturdy bread-and-butter pudding—both sublime in their own way, but meeting different needs for different palates...

Suppressing a grin at her fanciful foray into culinary metaphors, she chewed down almost guiltily on her lower lip. This was no time for levity. God knew she'd been in dire straits for the past couple of years, and her plight had been only too serious... But right then Freya felt strangely inexplicably light—as though some of the troubles weighing so heavily on her heart had suddenly somehow lifted.

Stealing a glance at her serious-faced companion, able to explore that firm chiselled jaw of his and those enviable long eyelashes at close quarters, she allowed herself a surprising and momentary fantasy. They could be any ordinary young couple, she mused... Husband and wife taking a romantic break away from their busy lives in London—going to a place they'd bought for a steal a few years ago in the Dordogne and done up bit by bit, just the way they liked. They were going to unwind, lounge by the pool, read intriguing novels upon which they'd eagerly share their opinions over a glass of good red wine, and companionably share the cooking of the odd meal at home together, while at other times they would eat out in local cafés or bistros. Charming little family-run places, where they would be made most welcome and then discreetly left alone to enjoy the most divine food and, more importantly, each other's company...

So deep in the fantasy had Freya allowed herself

to drift that she didn't realise she'd released a long, heartfelt sigh.

'Won't be too much longer now before we're there,' Nash remarked, turning his head to briefly glance at her. 'What were you thinking about just then?'

'What do you mean?'

'That sigh.' The faintest lift at the corner of his mouth denoting amusement, Nash gave his full attention to the road again, slowing the car on the approach to a crossroads and flicking his gaze towards the array of signs there.

'It's just nice to be away.' Shrugging almost guiltily when she thought of the compelling little daydream she'd just conjured up for herself—a daydream that was outrageous when she thought about it in the cold light of day—Freya moved her head to glance out of the window. 'I'm in the middle of nowhere and nobody knows I'm here…except you, my uncle and my mother.'

'Freedom,' Nash agreed.

'Yes—freedom. It doesn't happen very often.'

Not long after the crossroads, they arrived at the centuries-old renovated farmhouse that was Nash's favourite retreat in the world. Its solid stone and mortar well-rooted in the earth, it looked as though it had stood there as long as the land containing it. The moment he drove the new-looking Renault he'd hired onto the huge expanse of gravelled drive and the scent of sweet herbs and newly cut grass drifted in through the opened car windows his body and mind seemed to heave a collective sigh. He undoubtedly thrived on the challenges and demands of his work, but he'd be a liar if he said he never felt like having the occasional break away from stressful city life.

Soon, with the sun blazing down on his dark blond head, Nash stood outside the engaging blue-shuttered façade with Freya, satisfaction and pleasure flowing through him at the thought of spending the next few days there, speculating if the stunning Dordogne valley and this gracious old house nestled within it would effect the same timeless magic for her that it did for him. She was, after all, the first woman he had ever brought there. In fact, he couldn't even recall mentioning its existence to any of his previous girlfriends. He'd always thought of Beau Refuge, as he'd christened it when the renovations were done, as his private and secret bolt-hole—a haven away from the rat race, and a place where he could unwind and enjoy his own company after days filled to the rafters with wall-to-wall people… But where else could he bring a famous movie actress and accord her some much needed privacy as well? This had to be the perfect place.

'You're a lucky man.'

He turned and met the full force of Freya's dazzling smile. Although her eyes were still shielded behind her glamorous dark glasses, Nash could feel the sudden unguarded warmth from her gaze practically drilling a hole in his chest.

'I wouldn't argue with that,' he drawled lazily, his

glance making an admiring reconnaissance of her body in a candy-pink shirt and pale blue denim jeans. Even though very little flesh was on show, apart from wrists and ankles, and even though her fairly ordinary attire was not provocative in itself, it couldn't hide the soft, undulating curves of the very feminine body beneath it. And, remembering the mouthwatering picture she'd presented when he'd walked in on her yesterday morning in his spare bedroom—red silk underwear and all—Nash couldn't help the dizzying electrical charge that zig-zagged like lightning into the pit of his stomach.

'How long have you had this place?' she asked, turning her face quickly away to re-examine the thick white walls and sky-blue shutters facing them.

'About five years now. There's a couple who live locally that look after it for me...Victor and Didi. They should have stocked the fridge and the cupboards for us, and got the rooms ready. Want to go in and have a look around? I'll bring the cases.'

'Okay.'

After depositing their luggage in individual rooms, and telling Freya to explore the place at her leisure, Nash went outside to sit in the sun on a cane chair beside the glimmering aquamarine swimming pool. Before he made the couple of calls he had to make on his mobile he let his glance scrutinise the vale of lush woodland to the right of him, followed by the recently ploughed fields to his left.

Whilst they'd encountered no problem of being

pestered at either airport they'd travelled from and to, Nash knew he could not afford to rest on his laurels and be lax in his vigilance. Even though this place was remote enough—and he'd driven on as many back roads as he could to get there—he still had to be on his guard for possible intruders. It only took one person to recognise Freya and report her whereabouts to a local paper and before they knew it they would find themselves knee-deep in picture-hungry paparazzi.

It would be a damn shame after getting her this far without a hitch, Nash reflected, spearing his fingers through his hair. He wanted publicity for her, yes… But he wanted it to be positive, upbeat publicity—and to achieve that Freya needed the chance to rebuild her confidence away from the invasion of cameras and people. And of course the barrage of abuse she'd taken from her malignant ex-husband.

Yesterday Nash had learned with satisfaction that Frazier had been stopped and questioned by the police on his arrival in Antigua, and issued with a strongly worded warning straight from Scotland Yard. Nash's contact there had been only too obliging, and had done what he could to illustrate to James Frazier that if he so much as tried to contact Freya again he would be recommending a restraining order with severe consequences. When he'd related the events to Freya— Nash had been gratified to see some of the fear that haunted her leave her eyes. Now his hope was that she would relax sufficiently to start seeing the myriad possibilities of living a far happier life than she'd been living of late…

In the middle of unpacking, Freya glanced out the tall shuttered windows that she'd immediately opened wide on entering the bedroom and glanced interestedly across at Nash, sitting in a cane chair beside the swimming pool. His tousled blond hair was a halo of dark golden flame, and his lightly tanned, fit body was clad in long ecru-coloured shorts and a white T-shirt. As he sat with his mobile phone pressed to his ear, Freya saw the sinews in his muscular arms flex a little as he moved, and her mouth went as dry as tinder.

Impatient with herself, she turned abruptly away from the too-disturbing sight of him and stood in the centre of the room, with its high ceiling, cool stone floor and neatly made bed, frowning deeply. She had no business ogling him like some starstruck movie fan, she chided herself irritably. In effect they were both at the farmhouse to work. Nash to get to know her with a view to helping her professionally, and she to seriously think about how she was going to proceed with her career.

Her little fantasy in the car when they'd been travelling earlier—about them being husband and wife—had been totally ridiculous and unhelpful. Freya wasn't interested in having another relationship—and, not only that, the mere idea of getting married again was enough to make her shudder. No…she would avoid entanglement at all costs, she decided firmly, and concentrate on making her future as good as she could make it, knowing that she was going to stay a single woman for a very long time.

But even as she laid her folded T-shirts and underwear into a lined drawer that smelled of lavender, Freya couldn't help wondering why it was that a man as dynamic and attractive as Nash lived alone. Was he in a relationship at the moment? she mused. Her hands stilled over the drawer to properly reflect upon the matter. Just because he lived alone it didn't signify that he wasn't seeing someone. Perhaps he had been married, divorced, or even widowed and at the moment was unattached? And what had happened to the daring beauty who had shoehorned herself into that outrageous dress at the party?

Before she knew what she'd intended, Freya found herself gravitating towards the window again, to rest her gaze on the man whose charismatic presence was so plaguing her mind. He'd left his chair and was now standing by the pool, gazing out at some distant viewpoint that she couldn't immediately fathom. As she continued to stare—her body only too intimately aware of the stunning impact of his tanned, golden good looks—Nash moved his head ever so slightly. In the next second he was staring back at her, his sensual lips unsmiling and his fathomless blue eyes locked onto hers as though he had discovered something far more compelling than whatever he had been looking at earlier to rest his gaze upon.

Hurriedly moving away from the window, Freya

suddenly felt as if her limbs had lost all their strength and she was standing upright by sheer will alone…

'What's that?'

'What?'

'That huge bird! It looks like some kind of bird of prey.'

'It's a heron…you see a lot of them round here.'

Reaching for his wine glass, Nash sipped a little of the dry red wine that was made locally and of which his rustic wine cellar contained a generous amount. They were sitting outside the front of the house, around an octagonal wooden table with matching chairs and a huge green umbrella they'd agreed to dispense with as the sun started to set. The air was swiftly cooling after a day of hot Mediterranean sunshine, but he was quite content to sit outside and bask in the scenery. He included Freya in that, and told himself he was only human.

She was wearing a pink thin-strapped sundress that showed off her slender arms and great shoulders to perfection. Never let it be said that a woman's shoulders couldn't be as sexy as hell, he thought with unashamed appreciation. Her sunglasses now positioned on the top of her head, she was squinting up at the sky—intent on watching the heron she'd spotted glide gracefully on the calm, still air. Just now she radiated the same excitement as a child who had discovered something new and fascinating—some amazing titbit of information that she could add to the growing storehouse of interesting facts and figures she was busy accumulating. He found himself smiling as he observed her.

'Isn't that an oak tree over there?' Lowering her glance, she pointed at a towering specimen just beyond the swimming pool.

'That's right.'

'I somehow expected the trees to be different to the varieties we have at home. Silly, I know.' She blushed and reached for a piece of baguette that had been left over from their alfresco supper. She had not, Nash observed, so much as touched a drop of the wine in her glass yet.

'You like trees?' he asked.

'I just love being out in nature.' She lifted her shoulders and dropped them again, carefully breaking some bread between her fingers, as if reflecting on something that belied the joy she had just expressed. 'Unfortunately my crazy life often prevented me from enjoying it as much as I would have liked to. I regret that.'

'Well, now you have it all on the doorstep. What would you like to do tomorrow after breakfast? Go for a walk? There's a little church not far from here that you might like to take a look at.'

'I'd love that!'

She had that little-girl joy on her face again, and Nash knew it wasn't just the wine that was warming his blood. Straightening in his chair, he settled his gaze into the same intense examination of her features as an artist about to paint her portrait.

'Why are you looking at me like that?'

'Do you have to ask?' he challenged.

'Yes, I do, as a matter of fact.'

'I'm looking at you because, inevitably, your beauty is distracting me.'

She dipped her head for a moment, clearly discomfited. Nash thought it seemed strange that receiving compliments might disturb her.

'Looks don't mean much at the end of the day…not really. I know the profession I was in doesn't really bear that out—especially where women are concerned—but it's what's on the inside that's important…don't you think?'

The way she asked the question made him realise she was anxious to have her view confirmed. Her insecurities about being accepted for herself were easy to detect. She didn't want to be admired for her looks alone. Freya needed to know that she was admired for the person she was. Nash didn't suppose for one second that her painful dalliance with James Frazier had helped her case any.

'True. But all the same I don't necessarily go with the "looks don't matter" argument. Everyone—man, woman or child—is engaged by beauty. You don't have to be defensive about the assets God gave you. They were bestowed on you…and the world…to appreciate.'

'That heron flying by just now…commanding the sky with such grace…that's real beauty.'

'Ever thought that he might be looking down at you and thinking the same thing?'

His teasing raised goosebumps on her bared skin, and Freya shivered. Not only did this man rob her of the ability to keep her mind on her train of thought, but his low, sexy voice, easily suggestive of smoky bar rooms and hot, no-holds-barred lovemaking in the most unconventional places, definitely drove the point home. Perhaps she shouldn't have so readily agreed to come to France with him after all? This breathtakingly lovely place that was clearly his own private refuge from the rest of the world was far too seductive to her already fascinated senses…as was he. Perhaps the situation—the two of them alone together for an indefinite amount of time in an isolated farmhouse—was simply asking for trouble?

'Aren't you going to drink your wine?' he prompted when she stayed silent.

Registering her untouched glass, Freya shook her head. 'I don't really drink much…just the very occasional glass.'

'No?'

'Don't you believe me?'

She was stunned by the intense wave of anguish that swept over her at the thought that he didn't. If that was the case, then why was he agreeing to help mend her reputation? Was it only to appease her uncle? If he thought she had a drink problem, as James had often told the press, maybe he believed she took drugs too? Her stomach recoiled in protest.

'I wasn't casting any aspersions.' Nash's voice was calm in contrast to the small riot that was going on inside Freya. 'But now that the topic has come up we do need to talk about some of the things that have been said about you in the press. If I'm going to help you then I need to know everything.'

'So you think I'm an alcoholic and a druggie? Is that what you're saying? What about a neurotic, demanding, crazy woman on the verge of a nervous breakdown? Do you think I'm that too?'

Jumping to her feet, Freya started to walk away from the table towards the house, but her desire for flight was halted when she felt her upper arm firmly commanded by a large forceful hand and she was hauled back to face a suddenly not so benign-looking Nash. Even when he dropped her arm her feet remained rooted to the ground in shock.

'We're going to get nowhere fast if you can't have an honest discussion with me about this! I'm not accusing you of anything. I just want to know the truth so that I can help you!'

'Are you sure it's not just so that you can judge me, just like everybody else has judged me?' she fired back, her dark eyes beyond hurt. 'Is your own life so beyond any taint of blame or scandal that you can have the nerve to act like some kind of moral jury on my past conduct?'

'I'm not looking to judge you! If you stopped being so damned defensive for a minute we might get somewhere!'

They were both breathing hard. Finally Nash dropped his hands to hips that were lean and straight as an arrow and sighed. As his glance regretfully roamed the expression of acute distress on Freya's face, he fired a question.

'*Do* you have a drink or drug problem? If you do then I have a responsibility to help you get some proper help to deal with it.'

'You mean rehab?'

At the look of resignation that appeared Nash couldn't deny the bolt of alarm that ricocheted through him. Following that, there was the sensation of utter bone-crushing disappointment. He had so hoped that everyone had been wrong about the drink and drug label that Freya had been tagged with, but now it seemed that the speculation in the press had some foundation after all…

God knew his own past was hardly without taint, and he might indeed be standing in judgement—but only because he believed that she was in effect throwing her incredible ability down the toilet if she was an addict of any kind. No matter how bad things had been for Nash in the past he had never resorted to drugs—medicinal or otherwise—to ease his pain…

'So you *do* have a problem?' Shaking his head, he started to walk away a short distance, thinking hard in the twilight.

'I don't take anything other than the odd paracetamol for period pains,' Freya asserted quietly behind him.

Turning to regard her, Nash saw her beautiful dark eyes glisten with tears. His mouth felt dry as gravel and sawdust combined at the sight.

'I barely touch alcohol and I have never in my life

smoked dope or snorted cocaine or done anything similar. My ex-husband, however, spent a frightening amount of our money on all those things. What I'm telling you is absolutely true. If you feel the need—why don't you come up and search my room? Just in case I managed to smuggle drugs on the way out here and have a secret stash squirrelled away!' Walking right up to him, Freya prodded her finger into Nash's chest. 'After all...I would hate to think that your own whiter than white reputation was in any way sullied by your association with such a loser as me!'

'Hey!' His hand locked onto her wrist as she spun away and held her tight. Before he could get out the words that were furiously backing up in his brain, pure primal instinct took over and he kissed her instead. For a moment she was soft and compliant in Nash's arms, and he felt her sag against him almost in a kind of hungry relief.

A passionately arresting moan escaped her—the sound raising all the hairs on the surface of his skin— and then, just as he warmed to the provocative sweet- ness of her satin-textured lips and the taste of her tongue swirling hotly against his own, she ripped her mouth away, pushing at him hard with both hands to put some distance between them. Her breasts were straining against the thin cotton of her dress with each agitated breath, and her dark eyes were flashing angry sparks of barely contained indignation.

'How dare you? Just what did you think you were doing?'

'In any language I think it would be easily understood that I was kissing you.' A throaty, gravelly cadence
almost locked Nash's throat.

'Why?'

'Why?' With a wry glance from his azure-blue eyes,
he crossed his arms in front of his white T-shirt. The
action made the muscles in his biceps bunch hard. 'Put
it down to the heat of the moment.'

Staring at him, her agitated breath appearing to slow
down, Freya closed her lips against what she might have
been going to say and looked at him instead like some
kind of little-girl lost.

'I don't need to come up and search your room for
drugs.' He sighed. 'If you tell me you're not using then
I'm going to believe you unless I see evidence to change
my mind. All I was trying to do was ascertain the kind
of help you needed, so that I could put you in touch with
the right people. That's all. I want you to be in good
shape when you pick up your career again.'

'Oh.'

'Pact?'

'I'm sure you can understand why I'm naturally a
little prickly about the subject. Wouldn't you be under
the circumstances? It's perfectly horrible, having people
tell lies about you. And as far as picking up my career
again goes…well, we'll see. I don't even have an agent
any more—much less am I in a position to be offered
any scripts to read!'

'That can easily be rectified, Freya. I know plenty of

agents in the business. I could ring any one of them tomorrow and get you an interview. But first you need to unwind and relax, get yourself feeling good again.'

'All right.' Smoothing her hands down the sides of her pretty cotton dress, she looked distracted for a moment, as if she didn't quite know what to do next. Even so, Nash couldn't attest to regretting that inflammatory kiss they'd shared just a few moments ago. Not when his whole body was still craving her touch as though it were indeed an opiate he was becoming addicted to.

'I think I'll have an early night, if you don't mind? I'm feeling rather tired after all the travelling and everything today.'

Without waiting for him to comment Freya turned and went back inside the house, leaving Nash to murmur a heartfelt expletive to the rapidly cooling night air…

CHAPTER SIX

SHE couldn't sleep. When the dawn finally broke, Freya got up, showered and dressed, then sat quietly on her bed making a half-hearted attempt to read the book she'd brought with her.

Once again the words blurred on the page and, more than a little exasperated, she pushed to her feet and went to the window. Opening it with as little noise as possible, she drank in the sharp cold blast of morning air and let her gaze roam the beauty of the surrounding countryside. But her mind wasn't really on the sublime scenery. After Nash had kissed her so hungrily last night it was practically impossible to concentrate on anything else.

She'd been so mad at him…not for the kiss…but for believing for even one second that she was some kind of unstable addict. Then, just when she'd thought he was like everyone else after all—quick to judge her and point out her faults—he'd completely confounded her with that kiss and made her melt. Freya had still been shaking when she'd climbed the stairs to her room in the aftermath.

There was no way she could lie to herself and pretend she had been offended, even though she'd acted so indignant at the time. How could a woman not like a kiss that made her feel feminine and desirable once more after she'd started to doubt if any man would ever desire her again? Almost immediately her own hunger had risen to meet his, and the sheer desperate ache that had built inside her, so avid for release, had terrified her. If it had carried on she might easily have ended up in Nash's bed... A breathless little sound escaped her into the freezing air. Had she completely lost her mind?

Distressed, Freya turned away from the window and, grabbing up her sweater, draped it round her shoulders over the blue shirt she'd donned with a pair of white jeans, then hurriedly vacated the room to go in search of some coffee...

She didn't mention the kiss and, taking his cue from her, Nash decided not to raise the topic either. However, from the moment he set eyes on Freya the next morning—sitting outside at the table, catching the sun's first rays as she sipped her coffee—he was immediately aware of the tension it had wrought. It was as though he had transgressed an emblazoned prohibitive notice whose instructions had screamed *Keep Out*—but he'd paid no attention and committed the deed anyway.

Now he couldn't help cursing himself for his self-restraint being so badly knocked off kilter that he'd ended up kissing her as he had. Even though he'd been so aroused it had been painful, he knew it hadn't been the best of moves. And he certainly didn't make a habit of hitting on his attractive female clients. In fact he'd always made it a strict rule not to. Also, after his unwelcome suspicions about Freya's alleged addictions, practically ravishing her on their first night away together was hardly going to help engender the kind of trust they needed to forge between them to work together. From now on, he decided, his own behaviour had to be exemplary too. And if Freya proved to become even more distracting, then Nash would just have to give her as much space as possible, so that temptation would not be put in his way too often.

Considering he had to protect her from the paparazzi as well—it was going to be a hell of a tall order…

Later, walking across the fields from the house on their way to the small country church Nash had spoken about, he watched her lithe figure moving just ahead of him—her straw hat hiding her mane of opulent hair and her hips swaying almost too provocatively to be borne. He clenched his jaw as a trickle of sweat meandered down the small of his back underneath his shirt.

'You okay?' he called.

'I'm fine. This is great!'

'The church is just up ahead. There's the spire.'

When they reached their destination, Freya found to her disappointment that the ponderous oak door that led into the building was emphatically locked. Several huge rusting padlocks attested to the fact that it was no longer regularly used, and both the grounds and building displayed signs of elegant dereliction.

'Oh, what a shame! I was looking forward to having a look round inside.'

'How do you feel about graveyards? This one is pretty interesting.' Nash smiled.

Appraising the opened wrought-iron gates, and seeing the tombs looming up beyond them amid long grasses and weeds, Freya nodded. Removing her glasses for a moment, she wiped away the perspiration that had accumulated on the bridge of her nose and her forehead with the back of her hand. The day was warm and steadily getting warmer. It was a far cry from the overcast skies of the drizzly London they had left behind.

'Why don't you lead the way?' she suggested lightly—if only for the chance to watch him unobserved.

All morning she'd had a restless tension simmering inside her—ever since he'd appeared to join her for breakfast. Over fresh coffee, French bread, fruit and cheese, Freya had eyed Nash discreetly but helplessly as they'd talked and eaten, her gaze often alighting on that sensual carved mouth of his and remembering how delicious it had felt against hers, a jolt of hungry need flashing through her insides as she did so. What was astounding was that she'd scarcely thought about her past ordeal at all—or the fact that at home stories would be appearing in the newspapers about her again, after the interview she'd given. She'd even stopped looking over her shoulder, expecting paparazzi to jump out at her from some unnoticed hiding place. It was a revelation.

Now, following Nash into the churchyard, she found her attention reluctantly diverted by the presence of the large tombs that lay all around them. The ponderous stone cases were worn and weathered and strewn with lichen and moss, and several of them had pictures of the deceased family members entombed inside them, along with ornate tributes that included fake flowers fashioned out of plastic. An oppressive feeling started to gather strength in Freya at the sight of them, and she found herself wanting to leave. The realisation that they were family tombs slightly disturbed her—especially when she saw that some of the pictures were of children.

'It's too sad…can we go?' she asked, a betraying quiver in her voice.

'Sure.' Waiting for her to precede him out through the ornate iron gates, Nash frowned. 'I'm sorry if that upset you,' he remarked, his jaw set as he considered her from behind the dark shades that shielded his incredible eyes. 'I just thought you might find it interesting how differently they do things.'

'It was the pictures of the children,' Freya admitted.

'Yeah…I know. You like kids?'

'Very much. I always wanted to have at least three or four. I suppose, being an only child, a part of me always longed to have a brother or sister to play with. How about you? Do you want a family one day? Or maybe you already have kids?'

Nash couldn't fail to sense her intense regard behind the huge dark glasses. He couldn't deny the feeling of deep-rooted resistance that rose up inside him on the subject of having children of his own. He was thirty-six, and time was marching on, but he didn't know if he'd ever be ready to face the daunting prospect of being a father. The gut-wrenching experience of his own childhood as far as substitute fathers were concerned was enough to put him off the idea for life. And whilst Nash very much enjoyed women, and had had a few relationships—admittedly not long-lasting ones—he really didn't view himself as marriage material. Perhaps the truth was that he enjoyed the single life of a bachelor too much? Anyway…he had not met a woman so far that he wanted to share the rest of his life with. It interested him deeply, however, that Freya had confessed to wanting several children.

'I don't have any kids of my own, and I haven't really thought about changing that status quo any time soon,' he quipped, his tone wry.

'You're not—you're not in a relationship?'

'No. I broke up with my last girlfriend about six months ago.'

'Why?'

'Why?' Nash shrugged, slightly taken aback that she should ask him why. He didn't usually discuss his personal life with anyone—not even his mother. 'She wanted a bit more commitment than I was prepared to give,' he said truthfully, not liking the sensation of being suddenly put under a microscope, and slightly regretting that the truth had slipped out so easily.

'So…you're the kind of guy that likes to travel light, as they say? Isn't that how they describe men who have trouble committing to a relationship and like to play the field?'

As he registered the contemptuous tone in her arresting voice, a stab of anger shot through Nash. Where the hell did she get off, making such crass assumptions about him?

'Let's get back, shall we? Perhaps you'd like a swim in the pool instead of a walk?' He started to walk on ahead, down the deserted road that led back to the fields they had crossed from the farmhouse, and didn't spare a glance to see if she was following.

'You don't like talking about yourself, do you?' she demanded.

Nash kept walking, the back of his neck prickling hotly.

'My life is an open book—people can say whatever they please about me and that's okay—but you—you can't even have a decent conversation with me about yourself!'

He stopped. Slowly he turned, his hands on his hips, knowing acutely that she'd pressed a very hot button as far as his private life was concerned. Not talking enough about himself was an accusation that had come up time and time again in nearly all of his previous relationships. But to Nash his past was not some light aperitif on a conversation menu. It caused him too much grief for it ever to be included casually in an exchange.

THE READER SERVICE™
FREE BOOK OFFER
FREEPOST CN81
CROYDON
CR9 3WZ

NO STAMP
NECESSARY
IF POSTED IN
THE U.K. OR N.I.

'I didn't bring you here to talk about myself, Freya,' he said evenly. 'I brought you here so that you could get out of the limelight for a while and think about your future. When we get back to the house I have to leave you for a while, to go into town, but when I return we'll sit down and discuss some ideas. Deal?'

He was deliberately being all business again, and something in Freya baulked at that—even though he was right and that's why she'd come to France with him.

'What happened to the girl at the party?' she asked mutinously, whipping off her straw hat and pushing her fingers through the long dark mane of hair that suddenly tumbled like heavy silk over her shoulders.

'What girl?'

It was clear he wasn't exactly thrilled with the question—especially when he'd probably assumed he'd successfully deflected any more personal enquiries. Freya chewed down a little on her softly shaped lower lip before replying. 'The very clingy little blonde who couldn't take her eyes off you!'

'She was nobody important.'

'How flattering for the poor girl!'

'I meant that we weren't dating. She was just a friend.'

'Did she realise that distinction?'

'What's it to you?'

Freya shrugged. 'I was just interested to know if you ever brought her here to the house?'

Nash's body visibly stilled. 'I don't bring anybody out here but myself,' he answered.

Digesting that reluctantly offered titbit, Freya refused to be satisfied with such provocative fare without wanting more.

'If that's so…then why did you bring me here?'

'You needed some privacy…this was the best place I could think of to get you some. Any more questions, or are we done?' With the flat of his hand Nash palmed the sweat away from his glistening forehead. Freya had no doubt she had irritated him intensely.

'Don't you miss having someone special in your life to share this lovely place with?' She surprised even herself with her dogged persistence to weasel out more personal information about Nash's life.

'Do *you* miss having "someone special" in *your* life?' he shot back, turning the tables on her.

'After James?' Unable to ignore the sense of futility that the echoed question had provoked inside her, Freya crossed her arms defensively across her chest. 'No. Of course not.'

'Then let's leave the subject alone, shall we? We ought to be getting back…some of us have work to do!'

Watching him stride even further ahead of her, Freya swiped her straw hat against her thigh in pure frustration. 'Fine!' she muttered under her breath. 'But if you think you're getting away with not telling me anything else about you while I'm here…then think again!'

Sitting on a wooden bench that overlooked the valley, enjoying a clear, unhindered aspect of the farmhouse,

Freya watched another heron elegantly cut a swathe through the cloudless blue sky, then closed her eyes to listen to the mesmerising distant chorus of frogs croaking in a pond somewhere. It was very soothing just sitting there. Peace and relaxation had apparently found her at last, and she prayed that this time it was no fleeting visitor.

Sighing with contentment as the sun warmed her skin, she let her gaze drift with pleasure over the restful landscape once again. But her contemplation of the soothing scenery was suddenly abruptly banished by the sight of Nash, emerging from the farmhouse and walking towards her. He was wearing a loose white shirt over light blue softly napped denim jeans and his feet were bare. As he approached, sunlight glinting off the darkly golden strands of his hair, his easy hypnotic gait had Freya momentarily catching her breath.

'Ever read this?' he asked as he reached her. He was holding out a slim hard-backed novel, and for a moment Freya just stared at him without speaking, transfixed by the stunning intense blue of his gorgeous eyes.

Accepting the book, she pursed her lips a little to moisten them. Examining the cover, and at the same time acutely aware of Nash standing over her waiting for her verdict, she found her throat suddenly dry as sand.

'As a matter of fact I have, and I totally loved it,' she admitted with undisguised pleasure. Lifting her gaze, Freya steeled herself to meet that too-disturbing glance of his, just then feeling completely inadequate to the task. 'Were you offering it to me to read?' she asked lightly.

'It's been adapted for a movie and they're still looking for an actress to play the lead,' Nash told her.

They were adapting it for a film? Once upon a time Freya would have known something as significant as that. The fact that she didn't know only served to emphasise how long she'd been out of the loop.

'So?' But even as she endeavoured to sound blasé her stomach executed an excited cartwheel at the news.

'I think you should audition for it...don't you?'

'I told you...I don't even have an agent any more!'

'Why don't you have an agent any more?'

Shaking her head slightly, Freya splayed her palm against the smooth, glossy book jacket. 'Who wants to work with someone that's become a liability? Whose private life is such a disaster that she can't get her act together to even read a script...much less audition for a part in a movie!'

'Well...' His broad shoulders lifting in an unimpressed shrug, Nash stared down at her, his expression unmoved. 'Don't you think it's about time you started to get your act together? There's no time like the present. Why don't you start rereading the book, and later on you can tell me what you love so much about it and why you'd be the perfect choice to play the female lead.'

'I think your confidence in me is a little misplaced, if you don't mind my saying.'

'Actually, I do mind—because I think that's the

biggest load of rubbish I've ever heard! You could play that part standing on your head, Freya, and you know it! Why don't you stop juicing all those old negative beliefs you hold and show people what you're made of?'

Indignation surged hotly through her bloodstream at his unflinching words. He knew what she had been through, that there were still bruises smarting from her ordeal, yet he was calmly standing there telling her to get her act together and show people what she was made of! How dared he? She pushed to her feet and thrust the book back into his hand.

'You're supposed to be helping me! Is telling it like it is the tactic you're going to be using from now on? Only I didn't think I'd signed up for boot camp when I agreed to come here!'

'It riles you, doesn't it? Why didn't you act like this when your ex was busy trying to destroy your life?' Nash demanded calmly, his handsome face as implacable as she had ever seen it. 'Why didn't you stand up for what was yours? And I'm not just talking about financial assets here… Why did you let him strip you of so much?'

His words affecting her deeply, Freya felt tears sting the backs of her eyelids like a swarm of lethal hornets.

'I don't want to talk about this.'

'Why not?'

'Because your question is hardly fair!' she protested. 'You make it sound as if I invited him to treat me badly!'

'Did you?'

Once again Nash didn't pull his punches, and inwardly

Freya reeled from the impact. But this time she refused to take the easy route and avoid giving him an answer.

'All right, then! Maybe subconsciously I didn't feel I deserved the success I had… Maybe I was always waiting for the other shoe to drop, and when it did I just resigned myself to the inevitable. But I didn't deliberately choose to sabotage my life, you know!'

'But if you believed you didn't deserve your success then you did. We all make choices, Freya—practically every second of our lives. You could make the choice of wanting a better life right now! You could totally embrace the fact that you deserve success and that you're going to get it no matter what anyone else thinks! Maybe all you need to do is learn how to make better choices so that the outcomes of your decisions reflect what you say you really want?' Pulling his gaze away from her for a moment, Nash held up the book in front of her. 'This is an opportunity you can't afford to turn your back on. You're a born actress, Freya… I've seen you perform on screen enough times to know that's the truth. So do what you were born to do! Yes, you've taken some knocks—but what you need to do right now is dust yourself down and take up where you left off. Trust me…it won't be half as difficult as you imagine it to be.'

'And what about getting another agent?' Her heart-beat was picking up speed even as she asked the question, because she couldn't deny the realisation of possibilities that was excitedly building inside her. Freya accepted the book from Nash and felt her fingers close almost possessively around it. He smiled, and after the severe admonition he'd just dealt her it was like wallowing in blessedly cool rain after a drought.

'Leave that to me. All I want you to do right now is to start reading that book again. I need to drive into town to pick up some supplies for us. Later on, when I've returned, we can talk more in depth about things.'

'Okay.'

'Oh, and—' another smile provocatively hijacked his mesmerising lips '—you need a bit more sunscreen on your face…your nose is starting to get a little red.'

She'd been hoping that he'd been about to say something a lot more complimentary than that, and embarrassed heat flooded into Freya's cheeks. As Nash turned and walked away, she heard his throaty chuckle.

'Can't play the part of a beautiful Russian doctor with a nose like Rudolph!' he teased.

'That's what they've got a make-up department for!' Freya indignantly called after him, just before he re-entered the house.

Pausing outside the door, Nash grinned. 'Well…it's going to take a hell of a lot of make-up to cover up vivid cerise if you don't get that sunscreen on quick!' He laughed.

CHAPTER SEVEN

IT DID cross Nash's mind that he might have been too hard on Freya with his unsympathetic attack. But then he recalled the distinct flare of genuine excitement in her revealing dark eyes when he'd told her about the film part, and he knew that she had been as grabbed by the possibility of auditioning for it as he had.

He had taken a big chance, but he'd already got in touch with the casting agents on the movie and told them that Freya Carpenter might be interested. The agent he'd spoken with just happened to be a man whom Nash knew fairly well through his business dealings, and so was definitely open to some negotiating on his part. Even so, Geoff had been only too delighted at the idea of arranging an audition for Freya. He'd read the statement she'd made the other day in the newspapers, and he professed to be in admiration for her courage at finally speaking out against her money-grabbing ex.

'I always guessed the woman wasn't the total flake that Frazier made her out to be,' he'd declared emphatically.

Now all Nash had to do was keep on convincing Freya that this part—should she get it—was going to be the start of her long-overdue return to acting. His hands tightened perceptibly around the leather-covered steering wheel of the hire car he drove. Again he thought about the angry words he'd used to shake her out of her stupor of pain and regret. Had his anger arisen not just because he suspected she was still resisting taking total charge of her life but also because her situation so reminded him of what his own mother had gone through?

It was no secret that he'd felt bitterly disappointed and betrayed that she hadn't acted with more discernment in picking the men she chose to share her life— and Nash's—with. Considering that Freya might have acted with the same apparent lack of judgement definitely provoked a silent fury inside Nash. Yet at the same time he sensed that the actress had far more resolve in her little finger than his less assertive mother could ever dream of having. He prayed he was right about that.

Slowing down into the approach to the charming historical town, with its straight blocks of narrow streets and well-preserved medieval buildings, and finding an empty space by the roadside, he parked the car, got out, and started to walk up the steady incline that led to the picturesque town square, with its plethora of cafés and shops.

The afternoon passed into the evening, but Freya barely even noticed that the sun was going down because she was so immersed in the story she was reading. Nikita Pushkova had been a brilliant young heart surgeon at the top of her profession in Moscow when she chose to treat a poor child from the backstreets with a degenerative heart complaint, in her wealthy practice. The complicating factor had been that the child had contracted HIV from his prostitute mother, and just the mere association with that misjudged disease had been enough to send Nikita's reputation-conscious colleagues into a furious and indignant state of panic.

Going against the warnings and advice of her fellow surgeons, Nikita had operated on the little boy anyway, so touched had she been by his plight. Unfortunately, during the operation the child had developed an unforeseen complication and died. Nikita's reputation as an esteemed surgeon had been left in shreds and the hospital had fired her for bringing such disgrace upon them. The newspapers had inevitably got hold of the story and published a damning report about her that had effectively helped to finish off her career altogether. Her heart already broken by the fact that she hadn't been able to save the child, and seeing no hope of a future in the profession she had so passionately been drawn to, Nikita Pushkova had taken her own life.

The story had touched so many chords inside Freya when she'd read it the first time. Now, reading it again, she was even more deeply affected. But, more than that, she was absolutely determined that this part was going to be hers… If she won it, it would be the coup of her

career so far. It would also challenge her acting skills
in a way that they hadn't been challenged up until this
point. If Freya played this incredible but ultimately
doomed young woman then she owed it to her memory
to deliver a true and passionate portrayal of someone
who'd risked everything to save the life of one poor,
disadvantaged child.

She had just come to the end of a chapter in which
Nikita had emerged from the operating theatre, having
just lost the child she'd been so desperately trying to
save, when Nash called out to her. She'd heard him
return from town about an hour ago, but she had
remained sitting outside beneath the shade of an
abundant and gracious olive tree, totally wrapped up in
her book. Now, his announcement that dinner was ready
made Freya realise how hungry she was, and she was
on her feet and heading thankfully towards the house
with unashamed haste, her senses still profoundly
affected by the story that had so gripped her.

'There's apple juice if you don't want wine,' Nash
informed her as she pulled out a chair to sit down at the
rustic kitchen table.

He'd laid out a veritable feast for the senses before
her. There was an array of cold meats, pâté, fruit,
French bread and cheeses—including Freya's favourite, Camembert. For dessert there was a tarte tatin with
an almost full jug of fresh cream beside it. There was
also a carafe of red wine alongside the matching one
of juice. The mellow sounds of some sultry jazz played

quietly in the background, and the female singer's voice that accompanied it unashamedly oozed sex and seduction.

As Freya sat down, she was aware of an uncharacteristic sense of well-being and excitement flowing through her, and she realised it was nearly all down to this man. Just being in his presence seemed to energise her.

'You've been busy.' She glanced up and smiled. She saw a muscle tick in the side of his smooth-shaven cheek, and for one highly disconcerting moment he just stared at her without speaking. Then, as if someone had thrown a switch, he smiled back and the action created a cascade of delicious shivers that fizzed like sparklers all along Freya's spine.

'A budding Oscar-winner has to eat,' he teased lightly, pulling out a chair for himself.

'Yeah…' Freya raised her shoulders in a shrug. 'Dream on…' Her mouth tightened a little. Reaching forward, she helped herself to some bread and Camembert.

'That's what it's all about, angel…dreams. If you don't even allow the dream to take shape and believe in it then how do you think you're going to make it come true?'

'Is that how you got where you are today? By dreaming about success?'

'We're not talking about me.' The shutters came down again, and Freya tried hard to quell her sense of frustration.

'No…I sense a definite aversion to that. Do you think I'm going to sell your story to the newspapers or something, Mr Taylor-Grant?' she quipped, her dark eyes mischievous.

A knife-flash of pure unadulterated lust riveted Nash. The things this woman could make a man feel with that dancing, dark-eyed glance of hers were more potentially lethal than dynamite. All Nash's thoughts were directed to fulfilling the explosive desire that had all but blown his self-control apart, and every muscle he possessed quivered to contain it.

'Touché.'

Desperately trying to restrain the profound ache that imprisoned his body every time he glanced at Freya, he found himself wondering what it could hurt to talk a little about his own path to career success if it helped encourage her own dreams. Maybe it was the effect of the softly playing jazz, or merely that he was enjoying being a man with a very beautiful, desirable woman, but something was definitely prompting him to let his guard down a little. Anyway, he didn't have to tell her everything. He could be selective.

'I grew up in a one-parent family, and a ready supply of money and opportunity were assets that were hardly part of my life.' He cut some more bread and released a sigh. The jazz singer's voice flowed over him like a warm, soothing waterfall and helped him ease some of the tension that had inevitably cramped his chest at the mention of his past. 'Dreams of a better future were what sustained me even through the worst of times. I thought about celebrity and fame a lot in those days.'

'You did?' Freya's brows knitted together in surprise.

'Like many other kids I imagined those people who had made it into the limelight having the most amazing and thrilling lives. I wanted an amazing life too. But the more I thought about the qualities of fame, and the "specialness" it conferred on the people it visited, the more I realised the downside too. I only had to glance at a newspaper or magazine or watch the TV news to see that. Then I speculated that those celebrities must need good people around them to help deflect some of the not so attractive results of their fame, and I started to think about how I could get into something like that. There was a reasonable library in the town not far from where I lived, and I used to walk there every day after school and read the kind of books that I thought could help me. I also found an ally in one of the librarians there, who eventually suggested that PR might be the career for me.'

Grinning suddenly, Nash shook his head, remembering. 'I'm sure he thought I was either insane or completely living in cloud cuckoo land, given where I came from, but he gave me the information all the same. From that moment on I mentally worked on the idea of working in that field. When I moved in with my aunt, in a different, more...shall we say "well to do" area?...my dream really began to take hold, and there wasn't a day or night that went by when I wasn't planning my route to realising it.'

'You were a man on a mission...clearly.' Smiling up at him, Freya was almost intoxicated by the fact that he had shared this very personal revelation of realising his dream with her. She sensed it wasn't something he shared very often with people...if ever. The fact that he had clearly come from humble beginnings and had overcome his difficult start in life to become the success he was now made her warm to him even more.

'And you have to be a woman on a mission if you want to win the role that will be one step closer to winning an Oscar,' Nash replied. 'And you can't ever let doubt or what other people think get in the way. So...how did you get on with the book? Feeling inspired?'

Seeming to reflect upon the question, Freya leaned towards Nash with her arms folded in front of her on the table.

'A passionate story cannot help but inspire...do you not agree?' she asked him, in the most perfect Russian accent.

A hot charge of intense euphoria catapulted through his insides like a circus act shot from a cannon.

'So...you won't mind, then, that I went ahead and arranged an audition for you?' He grinned.

'When? How?' The shock on her beautiful face was a picture.

'You're telling me that you're interested?'

'Don't tease me...please!' She grabbed his hand and her warm palm curled around it.

Sweet heaven! Nash wanted to tease her some more—but not here. The teasing he had in mind should most definitely take place in bed, where he would be able to hear her sweet moans of pleasure as he did the things to her that his mind and body were so avidly clamouring to do.

'Have you really arranged for me to audition for the part of Nikita?'

Her grip on his hand didn't lessen, Nash noticed with almost dizzying satisfaction. Her perfume filled the air and deluged his senses.

'I have. But we'll arrange the timing of it when we get back to the UK and you're feeling ready. I've got Geoff Epstein's promise on that.'

'Oh, I could kiss you!' She lifted his hand to her sweetly warm lips and did just that.

The pupils of his blue eyes turned to jet. Before she could say another word he detached his hand from hers and walked round to the other side of the table where she sat. Gazing deeply into her captivated glance, he reached out and impelled her to her feet.

'Before you ask, sweetheart...I'm not asking for payment for fixing you up with an audition. But I want you to kiss me. I want you to kiss me because I think I'm in serious trouble if you don't!'

And she found her lips as well as her will vanquished beneath the possession of his burning kiss. Her mind couldn't have swum more dizzyingly if she'd been on a carousel. The way his body pressed tight up against hers, as though they were one flesh, left Freya in no doubt about his desire for her. Iron-hard, his strength and need exploded onto her senses like a crescendo of fireworks—and if that wasn't enough his intoxicating masculine heat seemed to elicit the kind of weakness in her limbs that only a serious fever would otherwise accomplish. Every part of him seemed made to entice and seduce her, and resistance never even entered her head.

So when Nash lifted his head, and his mesmerising blue eyes branded her soul with his name in tongues of flame, Freya knew the outcome of this inflammatory exchange between them was nothing less than inevitable. Keeping her hand resting possessively at his back, she felt her excitement make her tremble—hard.

'What about our meal?' she asked, her voice hoarse.

'Are you serious?' His wicked toe-curling grin was pure sex, and she shook even harder. 'I want you in bed, Ms Carpenter…and I want you there right now.' Possessively catching her hand, he drew her through the open doorway.

In Nash's bed, Freya discovered a sensual haven and the kind of bone-melting seductive delight that even her most secret fantasies had lacked the power to conjure up.

Beneath them, the sheets were pale cold linen—but they could have been satin, velvet, the most sumptuously exotic materials from a Bedouin market for all her entranced senses knew. Nash's warm, commanding mouth became both an instrument of delight and torment to her, because every time he withdrew it from her lips Freya felt as though he'd withdrawn some vital component that her very nature needed to exist. She found herself begging him for more of the same, and her huskily voiced pleas stunned her with the welter of desire and need she heard in their register.

His palms came into full, devastating contact with her bared breasts, and his fingers teased and seduced their sensitive tips as a musical maestro coaxed the most exquisite heavenly sounds from his orchestra. Her hushed urgent moans as she yielded to his riveting attentions fell upon the air like pearls of morning dew clinging lovingly to lush blades of grass. His skin was so smooth and warm, and the soft hairs on his well-defined muscular chest rubbed delightfully against her as he claimed the right to cover Freya's body with his own.

Her moans became even more rasping and urgent as Nash lowered his head and started to rain explosive little kisses down the whole length of her, right to the tips of her pearl-coloured toenails. Such devastating lovemaking was a revelation to her, and she wished that it never had to end. Arching her body with a surprised cry as his mouth found the most sensitive core of her womanhood, Freya sensed the room spin crazily once more. Pure sensation drowned her in its spell, as though the air was filled with showers of tiny diamonds that kept exploding onto her body like shooting stars. Her fingers curled tightly into the stiff linen sheet beneath her as his silken tongue made her climax, and the scalding surge of wild emotion that inevitably accompanied it brought her to tears. It was as though some dammed-up body of water had burst its banks inside her and was now moving unstoppably through every sense, cell and limb she possessed—as though its force would not be denied any longer.

Returning to examine her face, Nash brushed back her hair and glanced with concern into the dark eyes that glittered moistly back at him.

'I didn't mean to make you cry,' he said softly, his palm touching the side of her velvet cheek.

'You didn't do anything wrong… In fact…you did everything right. I just can't help it. This kind of thing doesn't happen to me every day.' Freya bit her lip to try and stem the threatened onrush of fresh tears, trying to form a smile at the same time. 'I guess I'm just used to a man taking his own pleasure and that's it.'

Hearing her softly spoken confession, Nash found her unexpected revelation profoundly touching. It saddened him to think that she'd never really enjoyed the act of making love up until now because her ex-partner had never given her that ultimate pleasure. But then he supposed that tallied with what he already knew about the man. He shouldn't be surprised. Nash had never witnessed a woman cry when he'd brought her to climax. He was beginning to see that there were many undiscovered shades to this lovely woman that he had frankly been quite unaware of. It made him want to become acquainted with even more of the myriad facets of her personality.

'Well, right now your pleasure is right at the top of my list, angel,' he asserted tenderly, then kissed her with all the voracious need that had seized his body, the desire he had been able to exert such control over up until then almost threatening to overwhelm him.

'Nash...' She rubbed the pad of her thumb across his mouth, and smiled as he gazed down at her.

He thought that he had never seen such a mixture of innocence and lust on a woman's face before, or even guessed at the torrent of feeling that sight might elicit. Capturing her wrist with his hand to still it, he suckled the thumb she had been teasing him with, then applied his teeth to the tender part. Feeling her hips rise towards his in surprise and hunger beneath him, Nash moved away for a few moments to see to protection, then slowly—and with devastating care—inserted his aching shaft deep inside the warm cavern of her exquisite womanhood.

She was tight and hot, and her sweetly enraptured moan shattered him as it fell on the hushed air. There was not another house for miles, and right at that moment it was as though the entire world belonged just to them. A gravel-voiced groan was emitted harshly from his throat. With increasing urgent need Nash clasped her hips even harder with his strong muscular thighs and drove into her, bending his head to kiss her breasts, her neck, her quivering mouth and her eyelids. Sliding his fingers through her glorious hair. He knew his delight in her body was beyond measure as he sensed her climax again beneath him.

He had waited for that satisfying response from her, but now Nash finally gave his own mounting desire wings and let it fly.

As he let himself lie against her in the aftermath, the combined heat they'd engendered making them cling hotly together, he listened to her heart beating wildly against his ear and knew his own easily matched it, beat for beat. His lips curved into an unashamed smile of acknowledgement.

'I didn't realise you had even more talents than I first suspected, Ms Carpenter,' he teased gently, leaning up on his elbows and laughing into her eyes.

At that very moment Freya knew she had walked to the edge of a pretty high cliff and was poised to take that final leap. There seemed to be no going back after what had just happened, and she knew it. Watching that devastating sea of blue sparkle back at her, she thought she had never seen another man more beautiful. He was incredible. Right now her will-power was teetering crazily—balanced on a knife-edge as she warred with the desire to let herself fall for him, utterly and completely.

'My dad used to say I had lots of talents,' she heard herself reply, wondering how that poignant thought had somehow permeated her mind when it was still reeling from the devastating impact of Nash's lovemaking. Probably the emotion of the moment had jettisoned it up from deep in her unconscious. 'He used to say that I could be anything I wanted to be and that everything was possible if I only believed it.' She sensed Nash's gaze narrow with interest. 'You would have found much in common with him, I'm sure.'

'What happened to him?' he asked quietly.

'He got cancer and died when I was six.' She shrugged, trying to will away the desolation that almost closed her throat at the memory—feeling the old gnawing ache of missing the man who had meant the world to her rise strongly inside her. 'People say that I was far too young to remember him that well—to miss him as much as I do—but they're wrong. I remember every detail about him—the way he looked, the way he spoke, the way he smelt—as though someone injected the memory into my very cells so that I would never forget him. He made me feel like I was the most precious thing in the world. When I was with him I felt so…so loved…you know?'

Nash didn't know, but he would have liked to experience the same from his own father if he had lived. People said that girls often subconsciously looked to find men modelled on their fathers in character and even sometimes appearance. Had Freya been searching for someone to love her with the depth of feeling her father had loved her with all along? If so, she must have been totally blinded by the true facts of James Frazier's nature to be so misled.

'Those big brown eyes would melt any father's heart,' he teased lightly. 'I'm sure that you were very easy to love as a little girl.'

'But not as a woman? Is that what you're saying?'

'I'm not saying that at all!' A bolt of shock slashed

through Nash's insides. Did she really believe that she was unlovable? Even the mere notion astonished him. 'Where did you get such an idea?'

Her gaze sliding momentarily away from his, Freya wriggled out from beneath her lover and moved herself up into a sitting position. Getting hold of the sheet, she pulled it up to her chest as Nash leaned back against the pillows beside her. 'Men only generally admire me because I'm a fairly well-known actress. They don't ever seem to see the woman behind the roles I play. Then…when they get to meet me…I think that somehow they're disappointed that the "real" me doesn't somehow fit with the fantasy they've bought into. I think that's why James was so angry with me. I refused to play along with the role of this amazing movie star he thought he'd married. The parties, the whole celebrity circuit—they were all things that he craved and I didn't. He often accused me of being the dullest creature on earth!'

'The man's judgement must have been seriously defective!'

'Everyone has their little fantasy…don't they?' She bestowed a look on him of such unremitting anguish that Nash sensed his heart constrict. 'And when it's proved not to be true they feel let down.'

Her ex was even dumber than he'd first suspected, he thought vehemently. If the fool couldn't see the glittering diamond that was the real Freya Carpenter then he must indeed be blind! The true woman was so much more than any character she might portray on screen or on stage, and far more compelling and enchanting. Any man in his right mind would be honoured to know her…let alone have her regard!

The depth of his own feelings startled him. 'Remind me why you married him,' he heard himself comment wryly.

'Why?' Her dark gaze riveted Nash. 'Because I have a spectacular talent for not knowing who I can trust, that's why! Either that or I trust too easily. Also…I was frightened of being alone. I never spent one lonely day in my life until my dad died. He used to say that he'd never leave me—and if you tell that to a child they believe you! I felt like he'd somehow betrayed me—not just deserted me when he died. Maybe subconsciously I expect every man to eventually betray me? Anyway… You asked why I married James. Well…when a good-looking, attentive man who professes to think the world of me then tells me that he loves me…I…idiot that I am…believe him!'

There was shattering hurt in her voice now, and before Nash could react Freya had slid across the bed, grabbed her jeans and started to pull them on with her back to him.

'I guess I'm just one of those gullible women who always end up with the wrong man—the type that the press is so good at mocking!' Turning her head, her dark hair spilling across her naked breasts, hiding them from Nash's view, she nonetheless easily commanded his gaze—stunned by her actions though it might be. 'You can't be a one-night remedy for all my unhappiness, Nash. I know that. And let's be real here too. I know that you don't really want any more of me beyond a little sexual recreation. So…nice as just now was…it probably wouldn't do either of us any good to repeat it.'

Picking up her shirt from the chair where she'd thrown it, she quickly shoved her slender arms through the sleeves and did up the buttons. Then she collected the discarded scraps of silk underwear that lay there too and balled them into her palm. 'I'm going downstairs to get something to eat.'

'Hold on a second! Sexual recreation, Freya?' Nash regarded her with furious disbelief. 'Is that all you think this was?'

'Well…tell me what it was, then, if it wasn't that?'

Freya stopped at the door, with her hand on the edge of the frame, and her expression was one of weary resignation, clearly anticipating the worst. Feeling both regret and great frustration, Nash was suddenly hesitant to try and explain feelings that right then were out of his remit.

He knew the exact moment when her interest in hearing what he had to say withdrew, even before he'd said another word.

'I thought so,' she said quietly, and pulled the door closed behind her as she went out.

CHAPTER EIGHT

KNOWING that Freya had just come through a pretty horrendous time in both her private and professional life, and would naturally be wary of other relationships as a result, did not help lessen the sense of failure Nash had experienced when she'd walked out of his bedroom, he reflected.

Nursing a freshly brewed cup of coffee the next morning, he stared out at the azure horizon through the open kitchen doorway, deep in thought. Okay, he hadn't deepened their intimacy by readily talking about himself and admitting some of his own issues…but was that really such a crime? He hadn't deliberately withheld information…at least not consciously. But he'd be the first to admit that dealing with emotions was not something he particularly excelled at—especially in relationships.

Now he considered that he had been playing a role too. One that he'd hidden behind—and not just professionally. The disguise had also encroached upon his private life, and that was why he rarely talked about himself with intimate partners. All they ever knew was that he was a successful businessman with a textbook-perfect past that didn't really exist, and Nash silently admitted that he had disguised his true background through feelings of shame and regret. He'd even sometimes fooled himself into believing the fiction rather than revisiting the truth.

The fact didn't make him proud. Freya was braver than him by far. Openly discussing her issues with trust, she had frankly told him that she feared any man she got into a relationship with would probably eventually desert her…just as she felt her father had done. At last Nash was beginning to get a true picture of her make-up, and he had to admit that it rendered her even more appealing to him than she had been already. She was a sensitive, caring woman—nothing like the brittle, self-absorbed persona in the picture the press and her ex-husband had painted for the public.

Remembering the highly provocative sight of her as she'd presented her back to him to dress, and the way her long hair had spilled like a black velvet waterfall across her breasts, Nash had to contain a groan as a strong resurgence of last night's heady desire throbbed through him. To lessen its hold, he got up and walked out towards the swimming pool. Settling himself in a cane chair, he silently and perhaps bitterly acknowledged that the sense of failure hadn't dissipated in any way. After all, it didn't make him feel too good to have a woman gaze at him

as if he'd just confirmed her worst fears about him…
especially when they had just made love.

Shortly after Freya had left Nash alone, he'd joined her
in the kitchen to finish the meal they hadn't even started,
and—just as he'd envisaged—conversation between them
had been stilted, punctuated by long, tension-filled
silences. Not long after that he hadn't been surprised
when Freya had declared she was going to have an early
night. But today, in spite of this new unforeseen tension
in their relationship, Nash had to focus on the reason why
they were here together. He was supposed to be helping
her build her confidence, as well as protecting her from
negative publicity and working on strategies to help her
make progress professionally—not having his own ego
deflated by imagined disappointment.

'I've finished reading the book. You wanted me to tell
you what I loved about it and why I think I'd be the right
person to play the lead?'

She'd stolen up on him on silent feet, and Nash
glanced up at her in a simple white sundress, her lovely
shoulders bare and her soulful dark eyes piercing him
with their melancholy and beauty. Once again he was
struck by how this woman commanded attention as
avidly as a spectacular sunrise.

'All right. Why don't you pull up a chair?'

The book in her hand, Freya did just that. With a soft
sigh she opened the slim volume and flicked idly
through the pages. Pages that already appeared well
thumbed and scrutinised.

'I love the story because it's about a woman who was only too human—even when to the eyes of the world she was a frightening success. Then she made a mistake…a mistake that came about because she wanted ultimately to do good…not bad. And she was doubly punished for it…both by outside forces and herself.' Sweeping her hand through her long hair, Freya lifted her gaze to Nash. 'I know what Nikita must have felt like when she lost the one thing she felt she was good at…the passion that had driven her life for so long. And I know what it feels like to lose the respect and support of friends and colleagues because they've judged that you've made a wrong decision…a "bad" decision. I know intimately how that feels.'

'So you really want to go for this part?' Inside Nash's stomach was a curiously hollow ache. He had judged her too…he couldn't forget that.

'More than I think I've ever wanted anything else…yes. When we get back home, will you arrange it?'

'Of course…that's a promise.'

'So…' Closing the book, Freya met his gaze. 'What shall we do today?'

'Do you want to get out of here? Go some place for lunch, perhaps?'

'Can we do that?'

Now passion was replaced by hope, and Nash realised how difficult it must have been for her, feeling as though she was a prisoner in her own home—unable to accomplish even the simplest outing to the shops or an appointment, too afraid to go anywhere in case she was pursued by an insatiable story-hungry press. People who were generally looking to present her in an even worse light than they had already…

'As a matter of fact, we can. I've got some friends in town who run a small bistro. They're good people, and I think I can safely say they won't be ringing up the local newspaper as soon as you set foot in the place.'

'But what about the other customers? I don't want to feel as though I'm some exhibit in a freak show!'

'That won't happen. It's a very small bistro…just two or three tables. Celine and Denis will agree to close it to other customers for an hour or two while we're there.'

Freya visibly relaxed. 'Okay. So we'll have lunch there. In the meantime, I think I'll take advantage of the pool and do a few laps.'

Rising to her feet, she was about to turn and leave when Nash lightly grabbed her hand.

'Is everything okay?'

'Everything's fine. If you're referring to last night, you can relax. I'm not one of those temperamental women who sulk when things haven't gone her way. We're both here for very good professional reasons…let's not forget that. We don't want to sully our time together with any personal awkwardness that will make it difficult to work together, do we? Can I have my hand back now? I want to go and change.'

'I just want you to know that I didn't take what

happened last night lightly.' His voice was a little gruff, and Nash recognised his own awkwardness at being unable to adequately explain his feelings…to make Freya realise he was sincere.

'You don't have to explain.'

She tugged on the hand he held, and reluctantly Nash freed it.

'I think I do.'

His words almost made Freya stumble. She'd been torturing herself with the idea that he'd made love with her purely out of physical attraction alone, and she hated the way that made her feel somehow unworthy of any deeper regard than that. Now, finding herself the intense focus of his penetrating azure gaze, she prayed he wasn't going to explain away what had happened with some trite excuse that would make her feel even worse.

'You're an enchanting woman, Freya. Much more enchanting than I think you realise. And I'm not just talking about the beautiful actress here…I'm talking about the woman behind the roles she plays…the real you.'

Her breath hitched a little as Freya slowly let it out, silently hoping, praying, that the deeply touching words were sincere.

'I woke up this morning with your scent all over my body and I didn't want to shower it off…I swear to God.' His hand lifted to lightly touch her hip in the thin cotton dress.

Freya felt as if she'd received an electrical charge so

strong it had rendered her limbs as weak as a newborn lamb's. She found herself fervently hoping he would continue to touch her like that…to tease her and perhaps seduce her as he'd done last night. It wouldn't take long for her to be ready for him. The thought turned her cheeks scarlet.

Just then a light, tantalising breeze smelling of sweet herbs and Mediterranean sunshine stirred a lock of his sand-gold hair and lifted it away from a brow that denoted strength and passion in equal portions. To her intense surprise, Freya glimpsed what she believed to be a provocative suggestion of vulnerability, and her heart squeezed at the sight.

'Could you handle me wanting to know the real man behind the public relations expert, Nash?' she asked softly, all her senses begging her to touch him too—to reacquaint herself with the reassuring iron strength beneath that silken golden flesh of his. His hand stilled for a long moment against her hip, then he slowly withdrew it. Freya held her breath, believing he was going to deflect her attention yet again.

'The "real" man?' His wide shoulders lifted in a shrug. 'Forgive me if I'm a little rusty at knowing who that is.'

'You can trust me.' Now it was her turn to catch his hand and hold it. Bending a little towards him, she rubbed the pad of her thumb over the fine golden hairs crossing the back of his palm and gave him a cheeky grin. 'I promise I won't break your heart if you tell me all your secrets.'

'Oh, you do, do you?' Before she could glean what he had in mind, Nash had turned his hand to grip hers, and with a firm hard pull he'd tipped her straight into his lap. 'What if I don't believe you?' he suggested seriously, his warm breath drifting over her mouth.

Astounded by the very idea that she might be possessed of the power to ever accomplish such a thing—Freya automatically closed her eyelids as Nash tauntingly touched his lips to hers and kissed her—all disagreement and hurt forgotten as she surrendered to the captivating moment instead...

Celine and Denis seemed enchanted by Freya from the moment they saw her. They were not the kind of couple who were easily impressed by celebrity or success either. In their late fifties, they had raised a large family and run a lucrative eatery for many years now, and were known to take people as they found them. But Nash could see that as soon as Freya started to chat unselfconsciously with them—about the restaurant, their family, and their much-loved historical town—she immediately endeared herself to the couple.

Watching her—seeing her laugh and smile and be so complimentary about the admittedly great food they were served—Nash realised she had a gift for bringing out the best in people. The warmth of her nature couldn't be faked—no matter how good an actress she was—and again he thought it was criminal how low she had been brought by her ex. But she had come on in leaps and bounds over the past couple of days, he considered, and now, with the promise of that all-important audition for a much-wanted film part, Nash saw no reason why her life shouldn't be entering a new, much more positive phase.

As for himself, he was finding it extremely difficult to be as detached as he should be where she was concerned. Even more so since they'd made love. With every smile that came his way, every provocative grin, Freya was threatening to break down every damn barrier he'd ever erected. Now he was jealous whenever her attention was diverted by anything else…and that included even scenery as well as other people. It disturbed him to realise how involved he was becoming. Up until now Nash had never let emotions dictate where relationships were concerned, and that was the way he liked it. It was a way of being he understood…a way to have most of the pleasure and almost none of the pain. Now Freya was pushing buttons in him that he hadn't even known he had, and there seemed to be no let-up.

'You look like you have a lot on your mind today.'

Her glance was slightly quizzical as she faced him across the bright red and white gingham tablecloth, and he noticed that the sun had brought out two or three very appealing freckles on her nose. His attention further diverted by her pretty mouth, he felt heat swirl like a small but lethal cyclone inside him.

'You could be right.' He nodded slowly.

'Are you regretting taking me on?' she enquired

lightly, but she wasn't quick enough to hide the doubt that crept into her eyes.

'Where did that idea come from?'

'Well…you've brought me here, to your own private little hideaway, and you can't even go where you really want to go because you've got to think of me. That can't be much fun.'

Remembering that smouldering kiss they'd shared beside the pool this morning, followed by the blood-stirring sight of her in a scarlet swimsuit, and then vividly bringing to mind the way those endlessly long legs of hers had been wrapped round him only just last night, Nash seriously wondered if there was anything else that could possibly have given him more pleasure…or been more 'fun'.

'I take my work seriously, Freya. It's my job to think of you twenty-four-seven while we're here together.'

It was his *job* to think of her? Already sensitive to the way words could hurt, Freya sensed something inside her die at Nash's coolly voiced answer. She could hardly believe he'd described their relationship in such a detached and unemotional way. If she'd been in any doubt before that her sleeping with him had meant anything, then she had just had those doubts thoroughly confirmed. She was just another job to him—nothing else—no matter how enchanting he professed her to be. She'd be purely crazy to hope for more from him. Trouble was…she guessed it was already too late to tell that to her heart.

'How admirable that you're so dedicated!' she said

sarcastically, her stomach wrapped in a vice of hurt. 'My uncle certainly chose the right man for the job when he picked you to help me, Nash!'

'Hell!' His riveting blue eyes glittered with frustration as he threw his linen napkin down on the table.

'Yes… I've been there too… Shall we go now?'

'Sure…if that's what you want.'

'I do.'

'I'll tell our hosts that you said *au revoir.*'

Turning away from her, Nash got to his feet and went to find the couple before leaving. As she waited at a side door that led out into the narrow alleyway, next to a bright, eye-catching watercolour of the bistro with its blue and yellow striped awning, Freya tried not to let emotion overwhelm her. She told herself all she had to do was hang onto her composure and remember that ultimately Nash was in her life to help her gain some positive publicity to rebuild her career—not to have a personal relationship with her. Their having sex—she wouldn't call it making love now, after what he had said—was just something that had happened, some natural animal instinct that had arisen between them spontaneously because of their enforced closeness, and probably a one-time only deal. Her main focus now should be getting herself into a good enough frame of mind to go for that precious audition—and Freya was determined she would win the part too. There was no doubt in her mind that it was the opportunity of a lifetime.

'Ready?'

Suddenly Nash was at her side, opening the door for her and placing a guiding hand beneath her elbow. Freya wished she couldn't so easily detect the heat and disturbing masculine scent of his body, because it made it so hard to stick to her new resolve to be cool and distant with him. But when she glanced at his too-compelling profile she saw by the rigidity in his lean, carved jaw that he appeared equally resolved to be aloof with her. Already low, her heart sank even further. She'd believed they'd been making such headway in their relationship, but now she could see she must have been wrong about that.

They started to walk down the quiet street. Most of the little shops with their typically French signs were now closed for the traditional lunchtime break, and they walked with notable space between them, careful not to touch, as though they were indeed work colleagues instead of one-time lovers…

'Freya!' The sound of her name on a stranger's lips pierced the air, and before she realised her mistake Freya had spun round to see where the shout had come from.

Suddenly she was surrounded by flashing camera bulbs, the lights almost blinding her with their white-hot glare, making her raise her hands to shield her face from their almost violent intrusion, feeling dizzy and disorientated.

A strong arm gripped her by the waist and Nash started to lead her away from the gathering throng, shouting furiously behind him, 'Give her a break, can't you?' followed by what Freya imagined must be the same sentence in fluent, equally furious French.

'I thought you said we could trust your friends?' she burst out bitterly as they hurried over the uneven path, her sense of betrayal stinging worse than a cut from a blade.

'This isn't Celine or Denis's doing…I'd swear an oath on it!' Nash's arm gripped her even more tightly round the waist.

Suddenly they were jostled viciously from behind. Lashing out to protect Freya from the frenzy of invading bodies, Nash was caught up in a tussle with two thuggish-looking photographers. Without his support she lost her balance and pitched helplessly forward onto the pavement. Her hands went out just in time to save herself, but she still landed hard on her knees. The impact seemed to knock all the breath from her lungs, and for what seemed like interminable moments she lay there on the cold, damp concrete, her heartbeat going wild and her knees burning with fiery pain. Behind her Nash let out a torrent of enraged invective, then he was urging her slowly and carefully to her feet as she heard the paparazzi start to head *en masse* in a joint sprint back the way they'd come.

Freya couldn't stop shaking. Her white dress was covered in dirt and stained on the hem with the blood that was oozing from her cut knees. Her smooth palms were also embedded with grit from the road.

'Are you hurt anywhere else?' Nash demanded urgently, his blue eyes hard with concern and his face grey as his hand curled tightly and possessively around her bare arm.

'I don't think so. Please…' Freya begged, knowing that tears were dangerously close. 'Just take me home.'

He'd taken her back to the farmhouse, tenderly cleaned the blood from her cut knees and put dressings on them, then given her some brandy to help her get over the shock. He could hardly believe what had happened.

As soon as he'd got Freya to go and lie down for a while he was immediately on the phone to Fleet Street in London and to press offices in Paris and Lyon to try and discover who had sent out the order to pursue her. Heads would roll…he was determined about that. The look on her stunned face when Nash had picked her up from the pavement would probably be engraved on his soul for ever. It had been a stunned reflection of immense hurt and confusion at being betrayed yet again by the human race. Not that Nash considered some members of the paparazzi anywhere near human after what had happened today. With the uncontrollable way they had behaved—like some bloodthirsty, unintelligent rabble—it was a wonder that Freya hadn't been hurt even worse!

Now he knew they probably couldn't remain where they were. If the press had found out their general location already, then they would more than likely already know the whereabouts of the farmhouse…isolated though it might be. No. It was time to get back to London. His heart acknowledged his deep regret about that, but then sheer pragmatism took over and he realised that he could protect her better there. Nash would be insisting that Freya stayed with him at his apartment on their return. There was no way he was going to let her go home on her own and face a similar rabble unprotected. Already he felt more than responsible for her suffering injury...

She'd packed her bags as Nash had instructed last night, sad on two counts. Firstly that he hadn't sought to comfort her in the way she ached for and still seemed to be keeping her at a distance, and secondly because she wished they could stay longer. The sunshine had been such a balm after the depressingly rainy skies of London, and she wasn't in a hurry to relinquish it. The beautiful rustic farmhouse and the lush surrounding valley had indeed represented a kind of haven. But yesterday a serpent had entered her paradise in the form of invading paparazzi, and if they tracked her down to the farmhouse they would give her no peace.

Now Freya's only consolation on returning to the UK was the prospect of attending the audition. The thought rang curiously hollow for a moment but she refused to pursue the reason why.

Arriving in the kitchen for breakfast, she immediately settled her gaze upon the stack of newspapers piled on the tabletop. On the other side of the room some coffee was brewing in the canary-yellow percolator, sending out a delicious hunger-inducing aroma, but there was no sign of Nash. Wincing a little at the pain, and trying to ignore the aching stiffness in her legs and forearms— the result of yesterday's fall—Freya picked up the top newspaper and scanned the headlines. She saw the photograph of her and Nash before she could comprehend the accompanying words. Distress was clearly evident on her shocked face, but it was Nash's heart-stopping visage that riveted her even more. The photograph had captured him with his arm tightly circled round her waist, and he looked both possessive and fierce. All the moisture seemed to dry up inside her mouth.

'How are you feeling this morning?' he asked behind her, in that smoky bar-room voice of his.

She spun round, her heart bumping against her ribs at the sight of him in faded jeans and a pale blue shirt with the sleeves rolled back to expose his tanned forearms.

'Like I've been knocked down by a runaway horse!'

'I'm very sorry about that.' His expression suggested her words caused him some pain.

'It's not your fault. It goes with the territory… I should know that well enough by now.'

'I got up early to go and get those.' Nash jerked his head towards the newspaper she was holding. 'I wanted to see what they'd write.'

'And? Wait… Don't tell me. No doubt it's something along the lines of "has-been actress falls down drunk in the street"!' Angrily trying to field the fresh wave of injustice that ebbed forcefully through her,

Freya knew that she failed miserably. Was there no end to this torment of mind, body and soul? Was she forever to be judged by everybody? Resigned, she waited for Nash to tell her the worst. Her French was fairly inadequate; there was just a minimal amount of words she understood.

'It's nothing like that.'

'Then what is it?'

'They're suggesting that you and I are lovers.'

CHAPTER NINE

'OH.' CLOSING the paper, Freya threw it down on top of the others. It was to be expected that if she was seen with a man—and a very attractive man at that—the press would have a field-day speculating on their relationship. The fact that what they were saying was true this time didn't help. It only served to remind Freya how foolish she'd been when she'd succumbed to making her relationship with Nash more intimate. Being such an intensely private man, no doubt he must deplore the very idea that the details of his supposed love life were now splashed across all the newspapers. Well, perhaps it would help him understand the sense of violation that Freya had experienced when it was done so carelessly and thoughtlessly to her?

'What does that mean?' His shoulders stiffening, Nash contemplated her warily.

'You probably hate the thought of your private life being pried into because of your association with me...don't you?'

'I admit that it doesn't exactly fill me with glee, but it could serve a purpose that would be worth it.'

'What do you mean?'

'It could help you with some good publicity at last. I hate the fact that you got hurt yesterday, but at least if the press are speculating about your love-life then they're not maligning you by suggesting you're a drunk or an addict or your career is all washed up. In fact it suggests that you're picking up the pieces again and starting afresh.'

'So what are you getting at?'

'What I'm suggesting is that we play along with them for a while. Let them believe that we really are having a relationship.'

Scraping his fingers through his tousled blond hair, he gave her a boyish, lopsided grin…the kind of grin that could break a woman's heart with destroying ease. Somewhere in the silence that followed Freya heard hers crack.

'And that won't cramp your style? What if you want to go out with somebody else in the meantime?'

Even as she asked the question her chest tightened in anticipation of his reply. She really didn't want to hear him tell her they'd get around it somehow. The mere thought of Nash wanting to see another woman hurt enough on its own without having the idea validated.

'I'm too busy working to see anybody else,' he answered, looking slightly aggrieved that she should even ask.

'Of course.' With a disdainful toss of her head, Freya walked across to the percolator to pour herself some coffee. 'I forgot…I'm just another job to you, aren't I?'

'Will you drop that? You're *not* just another job to me, dammit! I would have thought you'd have realised by now that this is not something I make a habit of— becoming intimate with the women I work with.'

'How would I know that?' Freya shot back. 'I've only got your word for it after all!'

'Are you saying that's not good enough?'

As she saw frustration and anger cross his handsome face, she despaired that they were rowing. Only yesterday Nash had been so playful, almost tender with her by the pool, and when he'd confessed that he didn't really know who the real Nash was any more she'd seen past the outward façade of self-assurance and success and glimpsed a more complicated perhaps wounded man underneath. A man who carried hurtful secrets he could not bring himself to share…

'Well…' She lifted a dismissive shoulder, even though inside her courage and resolve to stay immune from his powerful attraction was rapidly deserting her. 'I think we're in danger of forgetting what's important here, aren't we? Getting back to the point in hand, if you think it's helpful to act out that we're having a relationship— and you don't mind the personal intrusion—then maybe it would be a good idea? It's already splashed across the newspapers so…like you suggest…we may as well play along with it. Do you want some coffee?' She'd swiftly changed tack when she realised she was in imminent danger of revealing feelings that he would in all likelihood reject should she do so, which would leave her feeling like the biggest fool that ever was.

'No…I think I'll go for a walk before we leave for the airport. I'll be back soon.'

Watching him leave abruptly, and wishing he'd invited her to go with him, Freya couldn't help but feel inexplicably abandoned…

Nash knew that after the reports in the French newspapers they would more than likely be besieged when they arrived back in London. He was right. He'd arranged for a car to pick them up and take him and Freya back to his Westminster apartment, but from the VIP arrivals lounge all the way to where their car was waiting they found themselves deluged by photographers and reporters, harrying them for quotes and pictures.

Freya said nothing, as Nash had instructed her to do, and he was the one to give the press the answers about their relationship that they were so voraciously demanding. As he did so he couldn't help speculating on what—in their avid enthusiasm for salacious facts—they would dig up about his own past.

Determinedly stemming the doubts and fears that ebbed through him, he let slip the information that Ms Carpenter would be looking at film scripts again in the upcoming weeks, and hinted that she was naturally back in demand by interested casting agents.

Once cocooned in the luxurious passenger seats of the chauffeur-driven Mercedes he had hired, Nash witnessed the signs of strain on Freya's beautiful face from this latest brush with the press. He deeply regretted that their sojourn in the South of France had had to be cut short, and he only hoped that it had not set her back in any way in terms of rebuilding her self-confidence. If she was going to give this upcoming audition her very best then she simply had to pull out all the stops to help her do so. She couldn't afford any more setbacks.

But as he examined the sublimely beautiful features he had come to know so well, Nash's mind went back to that scene in the kitchen this morning, when she'd told him that they were 'in danger of forgetting what was important here'—meaning the reason they had been brought together in the first place. Her words had seemed to be drawing some kind of line under their personal relationship, and Nash couldn't deny that it had disturbed him greatly. He didn't fool himself that once their time working together was over he would probably never see Freya again. She'd be swept back into that glittering world that seemed to bring her both anguish and pleasure, that set her apart from the lives that most ordinary people led. And apart from the severe blow to his pride, Nash realised that her words had set in motion an even deeper hurt inside him…a sense of rejection that he deeply abhorred.

'That wasn't so bad,' he commented now, referring to the events inside the airport.

'No…they were a little better behaved than when we were in France.'

Her dark eyes seemed to flicker apprehensively as she considered him, and Nash had cause to wonder if his making love to her had made her completely doubt his integrity. Damn! He needed Freya's trust in him if he was going to help put her career back where it belonged. More than that…he needed her to know that he would never betray the trust she'd put in him.

'Do you think they really believed that we're seeing each other?'

'They'll believe whatever they want to believe… whatever helps them sell more newspapers. And if I'm not mistaken they'll have a car on our tail even now, following us back to my apartment. That should confirm the idea.'

'I can't stay there with you, Nash.' Her disquiet about the matter was evident. 'I know you said it was a good idea, but I think I'd prefer to go home. You have your work to do, and I have to prepare for this audition—whenever it might be. Do you have any more news on that?'

'I rang Geoff this morning, while we were still in France, and he's getting back to me later. As for you going home…it makes more sense for you to stay at my apartment. After all, you are my priority right now, and I can help you deal with the press as well as taking you wherever you want to go. You'll also be able to rehearse for the audition without any distractions, and I can even stretch to a little cooking if you prefer not to eat out.'

'What about my clothes and the things I might need from home?'

'I can go and get them for you… Just give me your key and tell me what you want.'

'And what about—what about if you want to entertain a friend? Won't I be in the way?'

Seeing immediately what she was getting at, Nash felt a flash of profound impatience assail his insides. 'I told you! I'm not seeing any other woman but you!'

'But this is only pretend, isn't it? You're not really having a relationship with me at all.'

'What are you trying to say, Freya? Are you telling me that you *want* us to have a real relationship?' His piercing ice-blue gaze left her with nowhere to hide.

'No,' she said firmly, her stomach clenching in protest at the lie. Succumbing to the need to retreat after almost exposing herself, Freya moved further down in the butter-soft leather seat to stare out of the window at the passing pedestrians and the shops that flashed by. 'Of course I don't! We both know we're neither of us a good bet for any such thing.'

'Yeah,' Nash agreed grimly, turning to glance out of his own side window. 'You've got that right.'

Nash had gone and collected the things she needed from home and brought them back to his luxurious apartment.

He'd also given Freya some long-awaited good news…
The casting agents wanted to see her for an audition
tomorrow afternoon, so she had in effect about twenty-
four hours in which to prepare for the coming interview.
She planned to spend the time reading some more of
Nikita's story, to refresh her memory about the character
and delve as deeply into the woman's psyche as she could,
to give herself a real fighting chance to win the part.

In the past she'd insisted on auditioning for every role
her agent had set her up for—even the ones that had
been hers for the taking—just to prove to herself and her
employers that she could definitely deliver what they
were looking for. Tomorrow she would be exhibiting
that same passionate dedication. But that evening, as she
curled up on one of the comfortable deep-cushioned
sofas in Nash's living room with her book, she couldn't
help but let her thoughts and her gaze stray from time
to time to the man in whose apartment she was a guest.

At home, his shoes immediately came off, she'd
noticed, and he walked everywhere barefoot, his shirt-
tails hanging loose over his softly napped jeans and his
dark golden hair inevitably awry where he absently
drove his fingers through it. Contrasting that much more
casual look with the precision-perfect façade of his
office apparel, she knew the two appearances were chalk
and cheese—yet both were defined by a strong,
dynamic sensual undercurrent that Freya couldn't
ignore. And he looked almost as good from the back as
he did from the front… His shoulders were strong and

broad, his back and his hips lean, and his legs long and straight, with taut well-honed muscles in his thighs. He also had a rear end that she couldn't help but drool over whenever he walked away from her...

He was currently ensconced in the bright modern kitchen, preparing some salad and a pizza for their supper, and from time to time—to Freya's secret delight and surprise—Nash whistled as he went about the task. It seemed incongruous to her that a man with such innate charisma should do something so ordinary and endearing as whistle while he worked. It stirred renewed pangs of longing deep inside her heart for the chance to really get to know him, and for him to get to know her. But, telling herself that that could never be—and, more than that, she'd be crazy to risk another relationship when her previous one had almost destroyed her—she withdrew her gaze from the kitchen doorway, and the occasional tantalising glimpse of Nash moving back and forth between the worktops, and determinedly returned to the pages of her book.

'I've been thinking about organising an appearance for you at a local children's home I'm involved with.'

They were sitting on opposite sides of the long chrome and glass coffee table in the living room, having just finished their late-night supper, taking their time over coffee, when Nash came out with this announcement. Freya's dark eyes widened to saucers.

'They're doing a fund-raiser for some trips to the

seaside next summer. The home is very near where you grew up, as a matter of fact, and I thought it would be a good opportunity to get you some very positive publicity. What do you think?'

'A children's home?'

'Yes.'

'Do you mind if I ask how you got involved with such an organisation?' Her interest quickening at the idea of Nash revealing something previously unknown about his life—Freya barely moved a muscle as she sat waiting for his answer.

Hesitating, Nash told himself he should have known that she would ask questions about his association with the home, and couldn't see how he could avoid telling her at least part of the reason why.

Sliding his palms down over his knees, he felt his resistance momentarily forgotten as he became captivated by the rapt expression on her face. Whenever she was interested in something her features lit up like starlight. As diligent as he was about keeping his emotions in tight check, Nash couldn't kid himself that it hadn't hurt when Freya had answered with a firmly voiced 'no' when he'd asked her if she would want a real relationship with him. It had inevitably pricked at that sickening sense of rejection he'd borne since childhood—when his mother had more than once brought another abusive man into their home rather than take the chance of raising her son by herself and putting his welfare first.

'Is it really so inconceivable to you that I might have some involvement with a children's home just out of plain humanitarian concern?' he asked, an unconsciously rough edge to his voice.

'I wasn't suggesting that I found it hard to understand. I was only interested that you—'

'I didn't have one of the most idyllic childhoods. I think I already indicated that to you before, so let's just leave it at that, shall we?' He almost had to force the words from his lips they were so repugnant to him. They couldn't help but reignite the pain of old wounds he was in no mood to re-examine. Pushing to his feet, Nash couldn't disguise his irritation. 'Happy now?'

Freya got to her feet too. The smooth skin between her perfectly defined velvet brows puckered. 'That you suffered in childhood? No, of course not! But if you're asking if I'm happy that you told me so, then, yes! I can't help but feel it's a huge step forward with you being normally so reticent about discussing anything personal with me!'

'Well, don't get your hopes up that there'll be a repeat.'

'Why not?' she challenged, her dark gaze latching firmly onto his. 'What are you so afraid of?'

What was he afraid of? Staring at her as a man praying for divine aid stared at a vision of an angel, all his senses deluged by her dark exotic beauty and his whole body aching to go to her, to demonstrate to her without restraint what he really felt and thought, Nash didn't have to search hard for the answer to that question. Yet still he shied away from it, pushing it almost violently to the back of his mind, telling himself that such a conclusion was not for him.

'Let's just stick with the subject we were discussing, eh? Will you appear at the fund-raiser or not?'

'Yes…of course I will! But why won't you tell me a bit more about why you got involved with the home…about your childhood? I'd really like to know, Nash.'

'You're persistent. I'll give you that.'

'You don't get anywhere in life without being persistent… You'd no doubt back me up on that.' Venturing a grin, Freya silently admitted she would use every charm offensive she could to persuade him to open up.

He grimaced, clearly not happy, but at the same time looking as if he might just relent. 'Okay.' A sigh escaped him, and he was displaying the resignation of a reluctant patient when forced to take disliked medicine. 'I was raised by my mother after my father was killed in a road traffic accident when I was three.'

'Oh…I'm sorry.' Unable to hold back her feelings of empathy at the realisation that Nash had also lost his father at too young an age, Freya didn't take her eyes off of him.

'We weren't well off, and my mother struggled to hold things together. Not very successfully, I'm afraid.' Threading his fingers through his hair, Nash glanced briefly at Freya, then away again, as if the memories he was recalling were still too raw to contemplate. 'From time to time she thought that being with another man might help improve our situation, but it frankly made things worse…a lot worse. The men she got involved with were total nightmares…the kind of walking disasters that mothers warn their daughters about. They used her and abused her and a couple of them beat the hell out of me too. One of them attacked me with a knife, and I ended up in hospital, having a blood transfusion. I was just fourteen years old. You heard enough?'

The blue eyes that were so mesmerisingly flawless glimmered with clear disgust, and Freya sensed her heart swell with pain, shock and regret at the trauma he must have suffered.

'Oh, Nash!' Natural instinct made her go to him, but she froze in shock when he deliberately moved away from her, his raised hand indicating she keep her distance.

'I'm not looking for sympathy, Freya. You asked me about my childhood and I told you. Now just leave it alone can you?'

'But—my God! Your mother's boyfriend attacked you with a knife? That's dreadful!' She twisted her hands together, distressed that he wouldn't let her comfort him—even though she knew it was many years too late for the boy he had been. What had happened to Nash made her own story seem like a fairy tale in comparison.

'I'm going out for a while.' He backed towards the door, barely looking at her. 'Don't wait up for me. I don't know what time I'll be back.'

'Don't leave, Nash. Why don't you just stay and talk to me?'

'I've done enough damn talking, in my opinion! Just go to bed and think about something else, will you? How about the audition you're going to tomorrow? You need to concentrate on that. I'll see you in the morning.'

'No!'

She was at his side with her hand on his arm before he could reach for the door catch and go out. He was staring at her as a wounded animal stared at a predator that had just appeared and cornered it—most of the colour seemed to drain from his face at the idea he might be trapped. It took every ounce of courage Freya had in her to keep her hand wrapped firmly round his strong wrist, but instinct told her she shouldn't let him escape this time.

'I just—' She swallowed hard across the lump in her throat. 'I just want to hold you, Nash… Won't you let me do that?'

She saw him grit his teeth, registered the stark mirror of pain that glittered back at her, and before he could shake off her hold moved in close to his chest, slid her arm round his waist. For a second or two he remained rigid as a fence-post, but then…incredibly…she sensed him relent.

'Oh, baby, I hate that you got so badly hurt… I almost can't bear it.'

Reaching up, she kissed the side of his rigid jaw, felt his stubble graze her soft mouth then heard the harsh sounding exhalation he made at the contact. Euphoria and relief washed over her in a wild torrent when he caught her to him and held her so tight that her breathing was almost compromised. Sliding his hand up behind her head, Nash stroked her hair as he brought her face down onto his shoulder. Freya knew she didn't imagine the shudder of emotion that went through him. She didn't think she would ever forget it…

CHAPTER TEN

PACING the plush air-conditioned waiting room of the West End casting agents where Freya was having her audition, Nash mused that his position was not unlike that of an expectant father waiting for news of his newborn. An hour had passed already, and he thought if he had to wait another minute for her to emerge from Geoff Epstein's gargantuan office he would honestly go nuts.

Pausing for yet another glance out of the window, he saw that it had started to rain again. Watching the snail-like pace of the traffic inching down the long narrow street below, he rested a wary eye on the pedestrian access to the front of the building. So far he hadn't spied any evidence of paparazzi, but he knew that if Freya's audition hadn't gone well she would understandably not feel up to facing cameras on the way out. He sighed. His need to protect her went way beyond a purely professional requirement. That was blindingly obvious. And after last night, the way she had held him and offered him the kind of comfort he had never allowed himself to receive before, he was a man in turmoil. But telling her the truth about his background had been cathartic as well. Something frozen for too long inside him was indisputably melting, and he felt like a changed man.

Following the events of last night, Nash also couldn't help reflecting on how he was supposed to withstand having Freya share his apartment and resist touching her. Every time he held her at the back of his mind was the realisation that one day soon his agreement to help her would be at an end and she wouldn't need him any more. Perhaps he should try and start to let go of her from now on, to pre-empt any further pain her departure might cause him?

The door to Geoff's office opened at last, and the woman who had been commanding most of his thoughts came out into the waiting room. She was wearing slim black trousers with a classic white shirt, a black fitted jacket and a minimal amount of make-up. With her dark hair swept up on top of her head and kept in place by a tortoiseshell comb her graceful appearance resembled that of a svelte professional dancer rather than a well-known movie actress. Catching the dark-eyed glance that gravitated straight to him, Nash experienced the most incredible pleasure explode like a skyrocket inside him. The sensation was getting to be a habit as far as Freya was concerned, he acknowledged, silently and broodingly.

'Everything okay?' he enquired, when she didn't immediately address him. Before she could answer, a large middle-aged man with black wiry hair, wearing a striped shirt and braces on his trousers, emerged from the room behind her. He made straight for Nash and heartily shook his hand.

'Nash! Good to see you, my friend! It's been too long. We must have lunch together some time soon. How's business? Still burning the candle at both ends? A rich guy like you can afford to take his foot off the gas from time to time, don't forget!'

The words burst from his lips like machine-gun fire, and Nash couldn't help thinking it would be a good idea if he drew a breath from time to time…

'That's good advice. Business is good… How are you doing?' The younger man's smile was far from relaxed, and neither was he in the mood to indulge in polite chit-chat, even though it might be good PR. All he was really concerned about was how Freya's audition had gone and how she felt about the performance she'd given. Watching him across the other man's shoulder, her quiet steady gaze revealed nothing of what she might be feeling.

'I certainly can't complain!' Laughing at his own joke—the plush offices with the signed movie-star photos covering its walls and the framed business awards a vivid testament to his own personal success—Geoff Epstein turned suddenly to include Freya in the general banter. Moving over to her, he put his arm familiarly around her slender shoulders and gave them a squeeze.

Immediately Nash sensed rage boil up inside him at

the sight. Another man touching her like that was anathema to him, and he wanted to rip her away from Geoff's side immediately. But he didn't want to scupper any chances Freya might have of winning the role of Nikita by a jealous display of temper. He was certain she wouldn't welcome it, and might just think he was taking too much upon himself.

'And business is starting to look up even more now that we've got this young lady on board to play the starring role in our film!' the casting agent declared with avid glee.

Shocked and surprised, Nash focused his blue eyes even more intently on Freya. 'You got the part?'

The briefest smile of acknowledgement touched her perfect lips. 'It seems so.'

'I've seen about twenty other actresses and I've got to tell you…there was simply no contest! The director and I were blown away by her performance! Freya is the consummate professional…born to play the role of Nikita Pushkova. And the backers and producers will be absolutely delighted to have her join us. Thanks a million for arranging for me to see her, Nash… I owe you.'

At the bottom of the narrow elegant staircase, by the door that led onto the street outside, Nash laid his hand on Freya's jacket sleeve to make her pause for a moment. For someone who had just won what could turn out to be a career-defining role, she seemed almost too composed to be believed. Especially when he knew intimately just how much that part meant to her in terms of resuming her career.

'Congratulations. You must be elated,' he remarked.

She wanted him to hug her…or at least appear far happier than he did at that moment. But his expression appeared a bare degree warmer than stone-cold marble, and Freya wondered if he wasn't already thinking about the next client he would be taking on and was simply mentally letting her go. The thought made her feel sick inside, instead of elated by her good fortune. She didn't want Nash to let her go…or to think about anybody else.

Last night, when he had allowed her to stop him leaving and simply hold him after his reluctant confession about his past, she had been suffused with an overwhelming feeling of love for him that had made her want to hold onto him for life. It had taken great courage to tell her his story, and Freya knew intimately that it didn't come easy when a person had been so profoundly and destroyingly hurt. She'd wanted badly to make love with him, but had sensed his need to retreat and recoup after what had occurred and so had accepted his ruefully offered goodnight and watched him go to his bedroom alone.

Afterwards, she had mourned the too-great loss of his hard, strong arms around her, and the scorching 'lock the door' kisses that she'd so willingly become enslaved by. It had felt as if he was locking her out by keeping her at such a distance—even though he had finally accepted her need to comfort him. Now her only consolation was the surprising revelation that she still obviously had what it took to be a first-class actress and had won this coveted role…in spite of all her own personal anguish. Seeing as Nash seemed so resistant to allowing her into his heart, all the passionate feeling she was capable of would simply have to be focused on delivering a portrayal of the beautiful Russian doctor that would be faithful and true and show everyone what an amazing young woman Nikita Pushkova had been.

'I'm so overwhelmed I can hardly take it in,' she confessed now, smiling tentatively. 'I think I gave a good performance, but it's not always easy to tell. Anyway…it's all really down to you that I'm in this enviable position. If you hadn't brought the part to my attention and arranged for me to have the audition I'd still be wondering how I was going to get back into the business.'

'You did it all on your own merit, sweetheart.' The endearment slipped out before he'd noticed, and Nash followed it up by gently touching his palm to Freya's cold smooth cheek. Seeing the startled look in her eyes, he wryly withdrew it again and held up the long black coat he'd been carrying for her. 'You'd better put this on,' he advised, even as she turned round to slide her arms into the sleeves. 'It's raining outside.'

'I wish we could go somewhere and get a cup of coffee to celebrate.'

A soft, regretful sigh followed this somewhat forlorn remark, and Nash thought, Why not? She was hardly asking for the moon to go and enjoy a cup of coffee in a café, like any ordinary citizen had a perfect right to do! Yet he knew if they started walking openly down the street it wouldn't take long for someone to recognise her, and then the press would descend on them like a swarm of avid bees round the last blooms of summer. He frowned…then grinned.

'Wait here,' he instructed, taking the staircase two steps at a time as Freya spun round in surprise to watch him. Returning mere minutes later, he triumphantly produced a short blonde wig and a purple velvet scarf, courtesy of Geoff Epstein's casting wardrobe.

'Ta-da!' He grinned. 'Go up to the ladies' room and put these on,' he instructed, pulling his own coat collar up around his ears. 'If we're only out for half an hour or so we should be able to get away with it.'

Sitting in a packed corner of a well-known coffee outlet just off Oxford Street, Nash watched Freya sip her frothy cappuccino with a pleasure that could not be measured on any scale that he knew of. She put him in mind of an excited child playing dress-up. She'd entered into the spirit of her disguise with real zeal—even affecting a Swedish accent that in his opinion would have fooled his own mother, who was from that country. Her lovely face—framed by ash-blonde instead of its usual ebony silk—was no less beautiful, and Nash barely touched his own coffee for looking at her instead.

'I can't tell you how much I've missed this!' She

leaned towards him across the small round table. If it hadn't been for the fact she didn't want to attract unwanted attention. Freya could have hugged Nash right there and then in front of everyone. Her delight in this small, not insignificant pleasure almost overwhelmed her. 'Thank you.'

'My pleasure. You're a knockout as a blonde, by the way.'

His voice was a little husky, she noticed, and the bedroom cadence of it made her shiver.

'Am I?'

'I'll have to get you to play dress-up for me in private one day soon,' he joked, but the laser-like heat in his crystal blue eyes burned her, and belied the humour in his tone.

To deflect the answering swell of need that arose like a deep wave from the bottom of a deceptively calm ocean inside her, Freya quickly sought a less provocative subject to talk about.

'When did you want me to do the benefit at the children's home?'

His answering glance was no less intense. 'It's on Saturday…just a few days' time. I'm going to speak to the press soon, to let them know you'll be making an appearance there. Did Geoff say when rehearsals start for the film?'

'Next month. We'll spend two weeks in London rehearsing before we fly out to Romania to look at some locations with the director.'

'It's going to be amazing for you.'

'I know.'

It was hard for Freya to rest her gaze on Nash and know that some time in the not too distant future he would no longer be in her life. She would be once more immersed in her film career, and he would be protecting and arranging more conducive publicity for another fortunate client who was overwhelmed by their predicament. The thought was almost too painful to bear.

She'd believed that living with the day-to-day misery of a failed marriage, a ruined career and a mercenary and cruel ex who'd bled her dry every which way was the epitome of despair—but it would be as nothing to the pain of parting from Nash now that she knew she was hopelessly, emphatically, in love with him. Her love genuinely was hopeless, since she'd now discovered that the dynamic PR executive was a man who clearly kept any suggestion of love away due to the wounds of his horrendous past. How was such a man ever to be reached?

'We ought to be getting back,' she said jumpily, needing to disguise the sorrow that had insidiously descended and stolen her joy.

'Sure. As soon as you've finished your coffee we'll go,' Nash agreed, his glance leaving her to diligently scan the room for anyone taking a too obvious interest in them, and also to check that there were no reporters or photographers waiting to pounce on them as soon as they set foot outside the building.

* * *

Both the children and the staff at the home had come up trumps. As the applause for the final act of the afternoon's entertainment died away—a charming rendition of *Snow White and the Seven Dwarfs,* no less—Nash speculated on what Freya had made of it. Judging by the completely enraptured expression on her face as she sat beside him on a hard plastic chair, she appeared as touched by the children's bright shining faces, and their determination to excel in their performances despite the heartbreak that went on behind the scenes, as he was.

Warmth crowded into his chest and rendered him almost too emotional to speak. But then Freya turned towards him, smiling her delight at the show they'd just witnessed, and Nash was struck again by how right it felt to have this amazing woman by his side.

'That was just wonderful!' she exclaimed with enthusiasm. 'I was astounded at how perfectly they all remembered their lines! Especially the younger ones.'

'They've been rehearsing for weeks to make it look seamless.'

'Well, it definitely paid off!'

A sense of hard-to-contain excitement was building up around them in the rows upon rows of seats occupied by children and staff alike, but at the back of the room the waiting press had been warned not to take any pictures until Freya actually got up to speak. Catching the eye of the principal of the home, Nash covered Freya's hand briefly with his own.

'They're waiting for you to say something,' he said lightly. 'Do you mind going up unannounced?'

'Not at all.' She started to get to her feet, a vision of slenderness and poise in her pink Chanel suit, her perfume lingering in the air with seductive tones of amber and jasmine. 'Wish me luck!'

Nash's answering glance was perfectly serious. 'You don't need it, angel,' he murmured, and his keen gaze was unwavering as Freya made her way gracefully up the five wooden steps that led onto the small wooden stage.

Her smile of greeting dazzled everyone present in that tiny hall—from the domestic staff and the children to the eager press and the principal of the home herself. She looked every inch the perfect ambassador of her craft. Something told Nash that Freya Carpenter would never, ever be the has-been actress that she had so derogatorily called herself when they'd first met. She had way too much talent and charisma for that ever to be a reality.

Her short but enthusiastic speech—praising the children's and staff's efforts and pledging her support for any future fund-raisers in whatever way she could— all but brought the house down. Cameras whirred and flashed and, agreeing to pose with the children, Freya put her arms around the eager little bodies that pressed forward for her attention. She seemed to have a special smile for each and every child there, clearly not just making an appearance to help further her career.

Nash realised she was genuinely happy to be there, and then—like a thunderbolt out of the blue as he continued to gaze at her beautiful joyful face—the truth hit him. In those few almost unreal minutes, when time seemed to strangely stand still, Nash realised he was in love. The realisation throbbed through him in a relentless tide of powerful emotion, and he shook his head in wonderment to try and relieve himself of the giddiness that had somehow seized his brain.

After that, it was hard to concentrate on anything but the need to be alone with her, to somehow convey his feelings…if it wasn't already too late. He had pushed her away so many times when she'd tried to get close. Would she believe his sincerity when he told her that he would never keep her at a distance again?

When it was time to leave, and they had said their goodbyes to all, he led Freya out to the car park. Oliver Beaumarche was waiting in the driving seat of his BMW to take Freya back to his house for drinks, then out to dinner. Nash was going to follow in his own car and join them. He wished that they were going straight back to his apartment instead, but his need to talk privately to Freya would have to wait now until they could be alone…as frustrating as that might be.

As members of the press spilled out of the home behind them, continuing to call out to her and take pictures as she stood obligingly by the passenger seat of the car, Freya glanced up at Nash with shining eyes.

'I loved the kids,' she told him unreservedly. 'I'd love to go back and visit soon. Can you arrange it?'

'No problem.'

'I think you're wonderful to do the work you do here,' she whispered, for his ears alone.

Nash tipped up her chin, knowing that the picture the two of them made would no doubt feature highly in the following morning's papers. And, though he couldn't help wishing that the intimate moment could have been more private, nonetheless he was elated just to be able to touch her. 'I think you're pretty wonderful too, Ms Carpenter,' he teased, then planted a soft kiss on her surprised mouth. 'You've made their day coming here.'

She smiled. 'Not as much as they've made mine.'

'That's enough for today, folks.' Nash addressed the small crowd round the car as he briefly turned to open the passenger door for Freya. 'Ms Carpenter has another appointment to go to, and I think you've all had plenty of pictures to be going on with.'

'Thanks, Freya! Good luck!' somebody shouted out, just before she turned and got into the car.

The car park miraculously started to clear. Seconds later, after a brief exchange with Oliver Beaumarche, who'd waited patiently for the melee to finish, Nash was about to say goodbye to Freya when a tall, skinny boy with a shock of raven hair and piercing blue eyes hailed him from across the other side of the car park. Nash glanced round, smiling in genuine pleasure as the youth approached.

'Hey, Mark! How are you doing? I didn't see you inside.'

'No. I should've been at school today, but I've been to an interview for sixth-form college. Why d'you think I'm dressed like this?'

Nash's gaze took in the slightly shiny grey trousers, dull white shirt and ill-matched brown flecked tie beneath the habitual grey fleece that was the only jacket he had ever seen Mark wear, and his heart squeezed tight.

'Maybe I thought you had a hot date?' he teased, a twinkle in his smiling blue eyes.

'Fat chance!' Visibly reddening around the jaw, Mark grimaced. 'Is that Freya Carpenter in there?' He stooped down with awe in his voice to gaze at the glamorous woman in the back seat of the Mercedes.

'Why don't you say hello to her, Mark?' Nash smiled.

Hearing the invitation, Freya held out her hand to the youngster. 'Hello, Mark. I'm very pleased to meet you.'

'Wow!' Shaking her hand and turning to glance up at Nash at the same time, Mark went even redder in the face. 'She's gorgeous!'

'You won't get an argument from me,' Nash replied without hesitation, his own gaze moving to focus on a pair of exotic caramel eyes that could all but make a man's heart jump straight out of his chest with one beguiling look.

Mark dipped his head a little towards Freya. 'Nice to meet you too, miss.' He let go of her hand and straightened again.

'Can I talk to you for a second?' he asked Nash, his expression uncertain.

'Do you mind?' Encompassing both Freya and her uncle with his glance, Nash put his hand beneath Mark's elbow. 'Why don't you get going? I'll meet you back at the house…I know the address.'

'Take your time,' Freya said easily. 'We'll see you soon.' She pulled the passenger door shut with a brief flicker of concern in her eyes, then sat back in her seat as Oliver drove the car out of the car park.

Leading the boy to where his own Mercedes was parked, Nash let go of his elbow and folded his arms across his chest.

'What's up?'

'I saw my mum yesterday…in the hospital.'

Mark's mother was a registered substance abuser and an alcoholic who'd spent time in Holloway Prison for stabbing her abusive boyfriend. Feeling his heart start to race at what the boy might be going to tell him, Nash squeezed Mark's bony shoulder beneath the shabby grey fleece.

'What's she doing in the hospital?' he probed gently.

'She's been using again, hasn't she?' Anger darkening his brilliant blue gaze, Mark dipped his head in a bid to control his temper.

In an instant Nash saw himself reflected in the boy's

condemning wounded eyes. Because rewind to twenty years or so and the boy standing in front of him could have been him. Hurt, angry, and feeling betrayed by the very people who were supposed to look out for him. Nash recognised the crushing, bruising emotions only too well. His own father had deserted him by dying and his mother…his mother should have protected him better, he realised with a shock. Why had she prolonged both his and her own agony by living with man after man who'd abused and mistreated her and her son? Wouldn't it have been better if she'd struggled on alone until Nash was of an age when he could have gone out to work and helped her himself? Why had she sent him to England, to an aunt he'd never even met before, to make his own way?

Slowly, he eased out a breath. She'd sent him to his father's sister in Essex because her thug of a boyfriend had almost stabbed him to death with a knife. The wound in his side seemed to throb and burn as he reluctantly allowed the memory to linger for a moment. But…in the final analysis…by sending him away his mother had perhaps done the best she could think of to protect her son.

'Is she getting help?' Nash asked the boy now, his fingers curling even more firmly into his shoulder.

'She's got a new social worker assigned to her case. Won't make any difference, though, will it? She'll still go back to drinking and using and there'll be another

low-life waiting in the wings to take her back home…
Same old story.'

'But it can be a different story for you, Mark.' Letting
his hand drop away, Nash narrowed his blue eyes as he
studied the pale, haunted face of the young teenager.
'You get into sixth-form college and then maybe even
go on to university—the sky will be the limit for a bright
boy like you. I've seen your grades, remember? I know
what you're capable of. And any time you doubt that,
or just want to talk about stuff, ring me. Here.' Taking
one of his business cards from his wallet, Nash handed
it to Mark. 'You want to know the best way to help your
mum?' he continued. 'Do it by excelling in whatever
you do. Be the best you can be and she'll be the proudest
woman on earth.'

'Suppose so.' Appearing pleased, but embarrassed,
Mark nodded his head at Nash's car. 'I'll do it too, if it
means I get to drive a Merc of my own one day.'

'Want to go for a spin now?' Nash asked him, feeling
certain that Freya and Oliver would understand if he was
a little later than expected getting to the house.

'You kidding? Oh, man, that would be cool!'

'We've got to clear it with the powers that be first.'
Ruffling Mark's thick black hair, Nash slammed the car
door shut and walked alongside the teenager back inside
the children's home.

CHAPTER ELEVEN

Freya had been wondering about the boy Mark she'd met so briefly before she'd left the children's home. Apart from his poor clothing, there had been a wounded look about him that had touched her heart. Noticing the way Nash had regarded him, with such interest and concern, had helped Freya see the indisputable goodness in the man she loved. Many people who had been hurt as badly as he had during their childhood instinctively wanted to retreat from the world somehow, and protect themselves from any reminders of the too shattering memories. But Nash had not behaved like that. He'd actively sought to use his success in helping others who'd had a less fortunate start in life…like he had had. She wondered if Mark realised what a potentially amazing friend he had in the older man.

Their dinner with Oliver at an end, Freya could hardly wait to be alone with Nash at the apartment. His gaze had scarcely left hers all evening, and a quiet but powerful anticipation was building inexorably through her at the thought that they might make love again. Her body yearned to feel his touch. Her skin was already hot and achy, as though she were incubating a fever at the mere idea.

When no press cars followed them from the restaurant, she felt like an elated escape artist who had pulled off a stunt previously thought impossible. At the apartment, after hanging his jacket on the chrome stand inside the door, Nash briefly excused himself to go and use the bathroom. Back at the restaurant a waiter had accidentally spilled red wine on his spotless white shirt, and he wanted to change out of it and put on a fresh one.

While she waited impatiently for him to return Freya wandered into the kitchen, then the living room, restlessly inspecting the immaculate, artistically designed rooms with an air that was definitely distracted. Selecting a Mozart CD to play on the state-of-the-art music system, she sat on the couch and shut her eyes to more fully concentrate on the music. They flew open again in surprise when the telephone rang. Hurrying to turn down the volume, she was just about to reach for the receiver when the answer-machine clicked into action. There was Nash's voice, telling the caller he wasn't at home and to please leave a message and he would get back to them.

A woman's voice, smooth and rich as opulent velvet, came on the line.

'Nash, darling… I'm so disappointed that you're not there! It's late in the evening, I know, but please ring me when you get this message. I miss you and love you lots, my angel. Speak soon.'

Freya had straight away identified the accent that filled the room as Swedish, and as the affectionate—she dared not think passionate—words echoed mockingly round her stunned brain—she levered herself off of the couch and found herself at the window that framed the twinkling London nightscape to such spectacular effect.

Nash was seeing someone else! Someone who spoke as if they were on the most intimate of terms! An acquaintance or even a close friend would hardly sign off their message with 'I miss you and love you lots, my angel'…would they? He'd lied to her.

Ice water seemed to seep into her veins as the terrible realisation sank in. It was just like a sickening replay of the horrible moment when she'd discovered that her new husband didn't love her at all and had only married her because of her fame and wealth. She and James had been at yet another tedious party and—his speech impaired by too much alcohol—he'd slurred the confession mockingly to a friend of his just as Freya had walked back into the room after visiting the cloakroom. But this was far worse than that repugnant memory.

Devastated tears slid down the softly smooth contours of her face and she cupped her hands across the bridge of her nose as though she were praying, catching them as they fell. How could Nash do that to her? How could he have made love to her—and he would have made love to her again tonight, she was certain—knowing that he was possibly in love with someone else? Was her judgement so impaired she could so easily be deceived by a man again? No wonder he'd sometimes seemed to keep Freya at a distance! No wonder he'd been so secretive about his past! He obviously had a hell of a lot to hide besides his background!

'Did I hear the phone ring?' he asked, strolling through the living room door just then, his hands adjusting the cuffs on his fresh white shirt.

Turning to face him, that chiselled arresting visage of his and tousled blond hair catching her on the raw, Freya strove to compose herself. 'As a matter of fact, you did. The woman who called left you a message. You'll find it on the machine.'

'Okay. I'm sure it wasn't important. I'll listen to it later.' His smile was relaxed and intimate, as if nothing could possibly be amiss, and as he started to walk towards Freya she could no longer control the turbulent emotion that was coursing through her at the idea he was seeing someone else.

'Oh, I would listen to the message now, if I were you, Nash,' she commented sarcastically. 'It sounded pretty important to me. The woman was practically desolate that you weren't in. And, by the way…she finished off by saying how much she loved and missed you! Who is she? Somebody you've been having an affair with, obviously!'

'What?'

Stopping in his tracks, Nash tried to assimilate the

sensation of driving head-on into a rockface at high speed. 'Of course I'm not having a damn affair!'

He was suddenly aware of the acute distress written all over Freya's lovely face, and saw that she'd been crying. His heart started to beat faster than an express train at the idea she believed he'd been seeing someone else all along.

'Then am I to deduce that it's quite *normal* that you receive phone calls late at night from some sultry woman telling you that she loves you?'

'Are you saying that she had a foreign accent?' Nash dropped his hands either side of his straight, lean hips and slowly moved his head from side to side in disbelief.

'Yes, she had an accent!' Freya burst out furiously. 'A Swedish accent, if I'm not mistaken! Why don't I play the tape and check to see if I'm right?'

Two things had hit Nash, like a force ten gale sweeping him nearly off his feet. Firstly, Freya had mistakenly thought his mother was some woman he was having an affair with…and secondly she was *jealous*! And if she was jealous then that must mean she cared about him…really cared. He hadn't left it too late to tell her that he loved her! If she knew how crazy he was about her then she wouldn't expect him to just walk out of her life now that she was on the brink of getting her film career back again. It was a revelation, and Nash's chest crowded with the kind of warmth that kindled forest fires.

'You don't need to do that.' He sighed. 'You're

right…the woman in question does have a Swedish accent. Her name is Inga Johannsson and she's my mother.' The corners of his mouth dragged up into a smile and he tunnelled his fingers restlessly through his inevitably mussed blond hair, hardly able to contain the sense of elation that was pouring through his bloodstream. 'That message you heard was from her. She was ringing from her home in Sweden.'

'Your *mother*?' He heard the doubt in her tone and for a few moments wrestled with the strongest urge to cross the room and go to her. He'd show her in no uncertain terms that she was the only woman he loved and wanted to be with, then he'd take her to bed and demonstrate it some more for the rest of the night.

'Why does your mother live in Sweden?'

'Because that's where she's from. Stockholm, to be precise. And until I was fourteen years old I lived there too.'

'And what about your father? Was he Swedish too?'

'No…British.'

Nash's heart swelled anew with the longing to go to her. He loved Freya. He had absolutely no doubts about that now. The thought of losing her made him experience the kind of dread he wouldn't wish on his worst enemy. She had become such an integral part of him that nothing in his life would make any sense any more if she weren't in it.

'Oh, Nash!' She ran into his arms then, burying her face in his chest as her arms twined tightly round his neck. 'I'm sorry I accused you of having an affair, but I was in pieces when I heard that message! Do you forgive me?'

Making her look at him, Nash gazed down into her passionate dark eyes with a slow, devastating smile.

'Yes, baby…I do forgive you. But you'll have to be very, very nice to me to make sure I don't hold any grudges.'

Freya's cheeks dimpled. 'How nice?'

'Come to bed and I'll show you.'

Taking her by the hand, Nash led her through the silent, spacious hall of the apartment to his bedroom. Outside the temperatures had dropped dramatically, and the sleeting rain that had been falling had long since turned to snow. After turning on a nearby lamp, the first thing Nash did was to close the blinds at the window and shut out the night completely. Then he returned to Freya and slipped her pink suit jacket from her shoulders. Laying it aside on a chair, he tipped up her chin so that he could see every contour and feature of the lovely face that was accentuated by the soft lamp-lit glow.

'I won't ever lie to you,' he asserted, and Freya sensed her heart stall, hardly daring to breathe. 'But don't expect me to go over every sordid little detail of my former life with you either. You already know some of the story, and for now that's enough. Right now I want us to focus on a different, far happier scenario…our own story.'

She loved him. Her heart grieved for every ounce

of pain and anguish he had ever suffered, but she understood enough of his character to know that it wouldn't benefit either of them for him to identify too freely or too frequently with the hurt he had endured. He had his own way of dealing with his demons and she had to respect that. All he needed to know was that it was Freya's heartfelt wish that they would meet any future challenges or hurt that came their way together.

How could I have lived alone all this time, Nash was thinking as he studied the beautiful face before him, and never realised how lonely I was until Freya came along? I never knew the thing that was missing in my life—the thing that could connect me back more fully to the human race—was her.

He hadn't told her yet how much he loved her. But he would. First he would take her to bed and demonstrate to her with every drop of passion and feeling he had in him how much he cared.

'Whatever you've endured, Nash,' Freya told him now, lightly pushing back a tarnished gold lock of hair from his forehead, 'you've obviously overcome to achieve what you've achieved. Look how much you've helped me restore my belief in myself...you should be proud.'

Remembering the boy Mark at the children's home, Nash allowed himself the faintest smile of agreement. Would he be telling him the same thing in a few years' time? He prayed that he would. In the meantime he would be proud enough to be his mentor and friend.

Glancing down at his watch, Nash smiled even wider as his gaze helplessly returned to Freya.

'I don't know how many hours it's been between kisses, but I don't intend waiting another second longer before I steal one.'

Angling his head to meet her lips, he kissed her full on the mouth, heat pouring through him in a blaze of hunger and desire as she opened for him and her tongue danced silkily with his. Then he led her to the generous king-sized bed that dominated the room, and with softly urgent sighs and eager touches they undressed each other and climbed beneath the duvet. Covering her delectable feminine contours with his own more hard-muscled form, Nash paid silent homage to her earthy, sensuous beauty. Then he showed her with his mouth, his tongue, his sex, just how much he desired her—just how much she had enslaved him and bound him to her with chains of love and passion. He intended to express that to her every day until they died…

And when Freya's sweet lips found that ugly ridged scar of his that was the cruellest legacy from his past, and kissed every inch of that seared flesh as though she were kissing the most beautiful thing on earth, Nash almost couldn't think any more for the powerful upsurge of emotion that arose inside him. Something broken in him seemed suddenly to reassemble, and he wanted to cry and laugh for joy all at the same time.

Later, after the storm of their loving, as Nash held Freya against him, her satiny behind pressed up close into the cradle of his hips, he covered her lovely breasts with his hands and placed a softly tender kiss at the side of her neck.

'Ever think about getting married again?' he asked.

Growing still at the question, Freya could hardly hear herself think for the sound of her own blood roaring in her ears.

'Think seriously for a minute about what you could be taking on, Nash,' she joked, biting back the sudden onrush of bitterness tinged with regret. 'James more or less left me stony broke. My house is mortgaged to the hilt, and I haven't earned any money in almost two whole years! And if you crave privacy then I'm hardly the best proposition for marriage, given the level of interest my life seems to invoke in the press!'

'I love you, Freya Carpenter. And I'd want to marry you whatever your life looked like! I didn't plan to fall in love with a gorgeous movie star, but hey…' she heard the grin in his voice '…we all have to make sacrifices in life…'

'Sacrifices indeed!' Turning round to face him, Freya was all but stunned into silence by the blaze of love directed towards her from those incredibly blue eyes of his.

'Just in case you didn't know…' he drawled thoughtfully, cupping her chin and drawing his thumb back and forth across that rather stubborn feature, 'given my own background, I'm hardly the most perfect proposition either.'

Warming to the subject, Freya snuggled closer. 'And

what can a less than perfect male specimen like you offer a far from perfect female like me if I were to marry you?' she teased.

'My heart,' Nash replied seriously, the fascinating hue of his eyes growing darker and deeper than a moonless night. 'Will that do for starters, Freya?'

'Oh,' she whispered, and for long, delicious seconds lost herself completely in his passionate and devouring kiss.

When she could finally bear to tear herself away from the delectably erotic promise his lips so tantalisingly offered, she gazed at him almost in awe. 'In case you hadn't already guessed…I love you too, Nash. And I'm not going to stop loving you…ever.'

'And when those adoring fans of yours try to trample over me to get to you, you can be sure that I'll be holding on real tight and won't ever let go.'

'Promise?'

'Promise.'

He pulled her round so that she was lying on top of him and proceeded to kiss her, until Freya honestly had no notion of being in the real world at all… Instead she lingered in a hypnotic sublime paradise that she never wanted to leave…

EPILOGUE

Two years later: Annual Film Award ceremony and dinner—the West End of London.

'AND the winner is…'

'This is your call, baby…are you ready for it?' Leaning confidently towards his wife across the glittering banquet table, where the candlelight lent even more of an incandescent glow to her alluring features than she possessed already, Nash felt his stomach clenched hard in a mixture of pride and emotion.

Freya had travelled so far to get to the unmatched position she held now in the eyes of the public and her profession, and nobody knew that better than he. Now she was a much admired and beloved actress whose star quality had blazed through when she'd played the incredible role of Nikita Pushkova, reminding the sometimes fickle viewing public just what this stunning woman was capable of. As soon as the nominations for the award of Best Actress in a Leading Role had come up,

Nash had not been the slightest bit surprised when Freya's name had featured head and shoulders above the rest.

Now, her dark, exotic eyes held his, as if she was terrified to look anywhere else in the crowded room, and she moved her lips in an urgent whisper for his ears alone. 'Please don't be so confident…I don't want you to be disappointed.'

But she needn't have been so cautious. People were already on their feet, cheering as her name was announced as the winner, and Nash immediately went to his wife's side and clasped her hard against him, in the shimmering red silk gown she wore, with its daring décolletage, kissing her full on the mouth in front of everyone before drawing back to bestow a tender, loving gaze.

'You did it, my angel! You *did* it! This is your moment, and I'm so damned proud of you!'

'I couldn't have done it without you.'

Her dark eyes were already swimming with tears, and she hadn't even made the podium yet! With her heart racing, and a sense of unreality the depth of which she'd never experienced before, Freya turned to walk the long red carpet towards the stage.

Accepting the coveted statuette from a handsome well-known actor, who'd flown in specially from the States to present the award to her, Freya was trembling so hard she almost feared she would drop the precious prize. Looking out at the sea of admiring faces, her gaze avidly searched the many smiling countenances for her husband's. When she found it, she let out a long, contented sigh.

'I feel like I've come back from the dead!' she quipped breathlessly, and the audience—already enchanted—cheered and applauded wildly. 'I won't say that playing Nikita has been the role of a lifetime, because I'm still only young, and naturally I hope to have a long and successful career doing what I love, but just the same it came along at exactly the right time—a bit like my husband, as a matter of fact!' She grinned happily, meaning every word with all her heart, and people cheered again. 'Nikita Pushkova was a truly amazing and inspirational woman, and I feel very privileged to have been allowed to play her in the film. I have so many people to thank, as I think you can guess, but before I do—' she once again searched for the arresting figure of her husband, resplendent in his midnight-black tuxedo '—there's one person I owe more gratitude to than I can ever adequately convey…my husband Nash, who did indeed help to bring me back from the dead and convinced me to resume my career when I seriously doubted if I would ever act again. He is the most incredibly good man, and two months ago—to add to our joy—I gave birth to our beloved daughter, Betsy.'

Her throat tightening at yet another display of delighted applause, Freya shook her head in disbelief at her own good fortune. 'I'm an incredibly lucky woman and I don't ever forget it. Nash…you and Betsy mean the whole world to me!'

Standing at the side of the glittering table with its

twinkling candelabrum, his handsome face visibly moved, Nash touched the tips of his fingers to his mouth and blew out a kiss towards the stunning brunette on the stage. He was the lucky one… He told her that every single night they spent together, and he would continue to tell her each and every night to come…

MILLS & BOON®
MEDICAL™
Proudly presents

Brides of Penhally Bay

A pulse-raising collection of emotional, tempting romances and heart-warming stories by bestselling Mills & Boon Medical™ authors.

January 2008
The Italian's New-Year Marriage Wish
by Sarah Morgan

Enjoy some much-needed winter warmth with gorgeous Italian doctor Marcus Avanti.

February 2008
The Doctor's Bride By Sunrise
by Josie Metcalfe

Then join Adam and Maggie on a 24-hour rescue mission where romance begins to blossom as the sun starts to set.

March 2008
The Surgeon's Fatherhood Surprise
by Jennifer Taylor

Single dad Jack Tremayne finds a mother for his little boy – and a bride for himself.

Let us whisk you away to an idyllic Cornish town – a place where hearts are made whole

COLLECT ALL 12 BOOKS!

FREE

4 BOOKS AND A SURPRISE GIFT!

We would like to take this opportunity to thank you for reading this Mills & Boon® book by offering you the chance to take FOUR more specially selected titles from the Modern™ series absolutely FREE! We're also making this offer to introduce you to the benefits of the Mills & Boon® Reader Service™—

- ★ **FREE home delivery**
- ★ **FREE gifts and competitions**
- ★ **FREE monthly Newsletter**
- ★ **Books available before they're in the shops**
- ★ **Exclusive Reader Service offers**

Accepting these FREE books and gift places you under no obligation to buy; you may cancel at any time, even after receiving your free shipment. Simply complete your details below and return the entire page to the address below. You don't even need a stamp!

YES! Please send me 4 free Modern books and a surprise gift. I understand that unless you hear from me, I will receive 6 superb new titles every month for just £2.89 each, postage and packing free. I am under no obligation to purchase any books and may cancel my subscription at any time. The free books and gift will be mine to keep in any case.

P7ZEE

Ms/Mrs/Miss/Mr...........................Initials ....
BLOCK CAPITALS PLEASE

Surname ....

Address ....

....

....Postcode ....

Send this whole page to:
The Reader Service, FREEPOST CN81, Croydon, CR9 3WZ